PUFFIN MODERN CLASSICS

Carrie's War

Nina Bawden was born in London where she still lives, but she is equally at home in Norfolk, where her mother was born, and in Wales, where she went to school during wartime evacuation from London. A year after she left Somerville College, Oxford, with a degree in Philosophy, Politics and Economics, she wrote her first novel. Since then she has written twenty-one adult novels and seventeen novels for children, most of which have been widely translated and adapted for film or television. The places she has lived in, and loved, London, Wales, Norfolk, Shropshire and Greece, provide the real-life setting for her novels. *The Peppermint Pig* takes place in Swaffham where her mother grew up; *Keeping Henry* is set in a farmhouse in Shropshire; and *Carrie's War* in the mining valleys of Wales.

Once you have finished reading *Carrie's War* you may be interested in reading the Afterword by Julia Eccleshare on page 171.

Other books by Nina Bawden

THE FINDING
HUMBUG
A HANDFUL OF THIEVES
KEEPING HENRY
KEPT IN THE DARK
ON THE RUN
THE OUTSIDE CHILD
THE PEPPERMINT PIG
REBEL ON A ROCK
THE ROBBERS
THE RUNAWAY SUMMER
THE SECRET PASSAGE
SQUIB
THE WHITE HORSE GANG
THE WITCH'S DAUGHTER

Nina Bawden

Carrie's War

Illustrated by Faith Jaques

PUFFIN BOOKS

PUFFIN BOOKS

Published by the Penguin Group
Penguin Books Ltd, 27 Wrights Lane, London w8 5tz, England
Penguin Books USA Inc., 375 Hudson Street, New York, New York 10014, USA
Penguin Books Australia Ltd, Ringwood, Victoria, Australia
Penguin Books Canada Ltd, 10 Alcorn Avenue, Toronto, Ontario, Canada m4v 3b2
Penguin Books (NZ) Ltd, 182–190 Wairau Road, Auckland 10, New Zealand

Penguin Books Ltd, Registered Offices: Harmondsworth, Middlesex, England

First published in the United States of America by J. B. Lippincott Company 1973
First published in Great Britain by Victor Gollancz 1975
Published in Puffin Books 1974
Published in this edition 1993

10

Typeset by Datix International Limited, Bungay, Suffolk
Set in 12/15 pt Monophoto Bembo
Printed in England by Clays Ltd, St Ives plc

For Margaret Gliddon

Carrie had often dreamed about coming back. In her dreams she was twelve years old again; short, scratched legs in red socks and scuffed, brown sandals, walking along the narrow, dirt path at the side of the railway line to where it plunged down, off the high ridge, through the Druid's Grove. The yew trees in the Grove were dark green and so old that they had grown twisted and lumpy, like arthritic fingers. And in Carrie's dream, the fingers reached out for her, plucking at her hair and her skirt as she ran. She was always running by the end of this dream, running away from the house, uphill towards the railway line.

★

But when she did come back, with her own children, the railway line had been closed. The sleepers had been taken up and the flat, stony top of the ridge was so overgrown with blackberries and wild rose and hazel-nut bushes that it was like pushing through a forgotten forest in a fairy tale. The tangled wood round Sleeping Beauty's castle. Pulling off the sticky brambles that clung to their jeans, Carrie's children said, 'No one's been here for hundreds of years . . .'

'Not hundreds, *thousands* . . .'

'A hundred, thousand years. A million, billion, trillion . . .'

'Only about thirty,' Carrie said. She spoke as if this was no time at all. '*I* was here, with Uncle Nick, thirty years ago. During the war – when England was at war with Germany. The Government sent the children out of the cities so they shouldn't be bombed. We weren't told where we were going. Just told to turn up at our schools with a packed lunch and a change of clothes, then we went to the station with our teachers. There were whole train-loads of children sent away like that . . .'

'Without their mummies?' the little ones said. 'Without their *dads*?'

'Oh, quite alone,' Carrie said. 'I was eleven when we first came here. And Uncle Nick was going on ten.'

Uncle Nick was old. He had been old for years and grown so fat in the stomach that he puffed when he stooped. The thought of him being ten years old made the children want to giggle but they bit the giggles back. Their mother was looking so strange: eyes half closed and dreaming. They looked at her pale, dreaming face and said nothing.

Carrie said, 'Nick and I used to walk from the town along the side of the railway. It was quite safe, not like an electrified line, and there weren't many trains, anyway. Only two or three a day and they came dead slow round the bend in case there were sheep on the track. When there were, the engine driver would stop the train and get out of his cab and shoo them off, and sometimes he'd wait so that everyone could get down from the carriages and stretch their legs and pick blackberries before they set off again. Nick and I never saw that, but people said it often happened. They were specially good blackberries here, easy to reach and not *dusty*, like at the side of a road. When they were ripe, Nick and I used to pick some to eat on the way. Not many, we were always in too much of a hurry to see Johnny Gotobed and Hepzibah Green.'

'*Gotobed?*'

'Yes, just like that,' Carrie said. 'Go-to-bed.'

She smiled. A remembering smile, half happy, half sad. Waiting for her to go on, the children looked at each other. Carrie was good at stories but sometimes she stopped in the middle and had to be prodded. 'People don't have names like that,' the oldest boy said, to encourage her. 'Not real life, ordinary people.'

'Oh, Johnny Gotobed and Hepzibah were real, all right,' Carrie said. 'But they weren't *ordinary*. Any more than Albert was. Albert Sandwich. Our friend who lived with them.'

'Lived where?' There were no houses in sight: the wooded mountain rose on one side of the old railway track and fell steeply away on the other. No sound of people, either: no cars, no aeroplanes, not even a tractor. Only a pigeon or two in the trees and sheep, baa-ing below in the valley.

'Druid's Bottom,' Carrie said. She looked slyly at the children and laughed when they laughed. 'It was really called The-House-In-The-Valley-Where-The-Yew-Trees-Grow, but that's a bit of a mouthful, even in Welsh. So everyone called it Druid's Bottom because it was at the bottom of the Grove.'

'No one knows about Druids really,' the oldest boy said importantly. 'All that mistletoe and human sacrifice stuff. That's just legend.'

'There's always a reason for legends,' Carrie said. 'It was certainly a Sacred Grove of some sort. Some old religion. Bad or good — I don't know. But it had a queer *feeling* — you'll see for yourselves when we get there. There's a spring that was supposed to have healing powers and the remains of what might have been an Iron Age temple. At least, Albert said so . . .'

'D . . . ah . . .' The oldest boy made a wild, gagging sound, as if a fish bone had caught in his throat. Then turned bright red and mumbled, 'How much farther?'

What he had nearly said was, 'Dad would have been interested in the temple.' His father had been an archaeologist, and he was dead. He had died in the spring. It was August now, and the first time they had gone on holiday without him. They had been driving through

Wales, to the sea, and Carrie had turned off the main road into a narrow valley and said, this was where she and Uncle Nick had lived for a while in the war, would they like to stop the night and see? They hadn't wanted to, very much; the little mining town was desolate and ugly and the only hotel smelled of stale beer and greasy chips, but Carrie had looked so different suddenly, so happy and ironed-out and eager, that none of them had said so.

Now, watching her, the oldest boy wished that he had. Her smooth, happy look was gone and she was screwing up her eyes and her mouth so that her whole face seemed crumpled. Like an old handkerchief, he thought. Perhaps it was only that the hot climb had tired her but it seemed more than that. As if she were, all at once, uncertain about something.

Her voice was quite steady, though. She said, 'Not much farther, I don't think. Of course it looks a bit different, places often do when you come back to them, but I *think* I remember . . . soon as you turned the bend and saw the tunnel – yes, there it is! *The first yew!*'

Between them, and the black, tunnel mouth, was a cleft in the mountain. A deep gully, dropping away from the ridge. No more ash and hazelnut trees with sunlight dancing and dappling between them, only the old, gnarled yews, growing thickly together. A dark green, silent place, where no birds were singing.

They stood on the ridge, looking down. The littlest ones pressed close to Carrie. She glanced at their faces and said lightly, 'A bit scarey? Nothing to be scared *of*, just a few old trees, though Uncle Nick used to be scared sometimes, on the way down. Oh, he *was* such a baby! He was even scared of the Skull, when Hepzibah showed him. And there was nothing to be scared of in that! Shall I tell you about it? It was the skull of an African servant who had been brought to England at the time of the Slave Trade. And it was supposed to scream if it was taken out of the house . . .'

The oldest boy resented her tone which was that of a grown-up amusing the children. He said, 'I know that sort of story! Screaming Skulls and all that! All rubbish, really.'

Carrie looked at him. 'Albert Sandwich said it was rubbish. He said the skull probably came from the Iron Age settlement. He said the British Museum would know. He wanted to take it and ask them when the war was over. He was interested in that sort of thing.'

She paused. 'Dad would have been interested too, wouldn't he? Albert and Dad were very much alike, in some ways.'

Although she was smiling there was something tight in her voice, as if she were holding her breath. Perhaps she was: she seemed to let it out in a long, gusty sigh, and walked away from the children, down the track to a place where a flat rock jutted out from the side of the bank. She stepped on to it and a little breeze caught her hair and lifted it behind her. She called out, 'There's the house. Come and see.'

They followed her and looked where she pointed,

through a gap in the yews. Druid's Bottom was a long way below them: a doll's house with tall chimneys, tucked in a fold of the valley as if in the crook of an elbow.

'There's a path,' Carrie's daughter said. 'A bit slippy and slimy, but we could go down if you like.'

Carrie shook her head. 'There's no point. No one lives there. No one could live there now.'

They looked again. 'It's a ruin,' the oldest boy said.

'Yes,' Carrie said. She sounded flat and dull. As if she had known this all along but had hoped something different.

'We could go down, all the same.'

'Though it 'ud be a long way back *up*.'

'Lazy. Fat, lazy tyke.'

'Fat an' lazy yourself with brass knobs on. Come on, let's go down then, it's not far.'

'*No*,' Carrie snapped. Her own sharpness seemed to surprise her. Hand flying to mouth, she gave a queer, trembly laugh and looked at her children. They stared back and saw the colour come and go in her face. She took a pair of dark glasses out of her pocket and put them on. Eyes safely hidden, she said, 'I'm sorry, I can't. I really can't. Really.'

That odd laugh again. Almost like crying. 'Oh, I'm so sorry. Dragging you all this way in this heat. So silly, really. But I wanted to show you – and to see for myself just once more. We were so happy here, Nick and I. I thought – I *hoped* that was all I'd remember.'

The children were silent. They didn't know what

she was talking about but they could feel she was frightened. Their mother was frightened and this frightened *them*.

She saw it. She drew a deep breath and smiled at them shakily. 'I'm so sorry, darlings. It's all right. I'm all right now.'

Far from all right, the oldest boy thought. He took her hand and said, 'Let's go back now. Let's go back and have tea.'

He drove the others on ahead with a look. Following them, Carrie stumbled, as if blind behind her dark glasses, but he held her hand tightly. It felt cold to his fingers. He said, 'Won't take us long to get back. Quicker, going downhill. And a nice cup of tea'll make you feel better. I suppose they will give us tea at that pub? Though it's not much of a place, is it? Neither the pub, nor the town.'

Derelict, he had thought when they drove through the main street. All those boarded-up shops and only old people about, dreaming on doorsteps or creeping along in the sun. Like a place that was waiting to die.

'Pit's closed,' Carrie said. 'They opened it up during the war but the seams were too deep. Not economical. I suppose once we didn't need the coal so badly they closed the mine down, then the railway. I should have known, really.'

She spoke as if she should have known more about more than the dying town. She sighed and he felt her hand shiver. She said, 'Places change more than people, perhaps. You don't change, you know, growing older.

I thought I *had* changed, that I'd feel differently now. After all, what happened wasn't my fault, *couldn't* have been, it just didn't make sense. That's what I've been telling myself all these years, but sense doesn't come into it, can't change how you *feel*. I did a dreadful thing, the worst thing of my life, when I was twelve and a half years old, or I feel that I did, and nothing can change it . . .'

Couldn't change what? He longed to know what she meant, what dreadful thing she had done – it sounded more interesting, to his mind, than Druids or Screaming Skulls – but didn't dare ask her. She had been speaking, it seemed, more to herself than to him; she might feel he shouldn't have listened. She would tell him in her own time. Or she wouldn't.

She was looking too tired to talk anyway. Tired to death, and so white. He thought – *I wish Dad was here!* And then, that if he could walk with his eyes shut all the way back to the town, it might magick him back. Crazy, of course – if he had caught any of the others doing such a crazy thing he would have laughed himself sick! But they were a long way ahead now, and his mother would never guess what he was up to. She might not think she had changed but she was too old for *that*! He would just walk on, holding her hand and letting her lead him, turning his head a bit so she wouldn't see his closed eyes and keeping the sun on his left cheek as an additional guide. The tricky part would come when they had to leave the straight track and turn down through a gate and a field, but magic never

worked if the thing you had to do was too easy. And if
he managed to do it without her noticing, when they
got to the pub his father would be waiting there.
Waiting for them and smiling . . .

'What on earth are you doing? Grinning like an ape
with your eyes shut?'

He opened them, saw his mother's face smiling
down, and felt his ears burn. 'I was just playing a
game.'

'At your age? You'd have had us over the edge in a
minute!'

She was teasing him as if he were one of the little
ones but he didn't mind because she was looking happy
again. When she took off her glasses the sun caught her
eyes and made them flash like green torches.

She said, 'Look, now! You can see the whole of the
town from here.'

They had left the wooded slopes behind them and
the valley had opened out. Springy, sheep-cropped turf,
criss-crossed with dry stone walls, ran down to the
back yards of the houses. Narrow, straight streets; one
long, thin one, like a spine down the middle and short,
stumpy ones leading off, steeply climbing the hillside.
It was peaceful enough and the slate roofs shone in the
soft, evening light, but it was still a hideous place, the
oldest boy thought: ugly houses and black pit machin-
ery and smooth cones of slag, meanly dark against the
green mountain.

Carrie said, 'See that slag heap? The one over there?
We used to slide down on a tray, though we were in

trouble if *he* caught us, mind! Wearing out our good clothes or wasting hot water to wash them!'

'Who's *he*?' the oldest boy asked, but she didn't seem to hear him. She was gazing down at the town and smiling her private, remembering smile.

'That's the pub where we're staying,' she said after a minute. 'The Dog and Duck. And that building there, the one with the green roof, that's Ebenezer Chapel where we used to have lessons some mornings because there wasn't room for us all in the school. It was only a small school, you see, not big enough to take all the extra children from London. And here, where we're standing now, this is the *exact* place where the train always whistled when it came round the bend. A simply enormous whistle that echoed in the valley. More like a volcano erupting than a steam engine blowing its top, Nick always said, but he was touchy about it because it made him sick the first time. Though of course it wasn't only the whistle. It was partly because he was tired and unhappy, leaving home and our mother for the first time . . .' She seemed to think about that for a moment – how sad it had been – and then started to laugh. 'But it was mostly because he had eaten so much. He really was quite dreadfully greedy when he was young.'

'Still is,' the oldest boy said. 'What's new about that? Get on with the *story*.'

'I'm *trying* to,' Carrie said, so impatiently that she sounded, he thought, more like a cross girl his own age than his mother. 'But the story *starts* with Uncle Nick being sick . . .'

CHAPTER 2

*H*e threw up all over Miss Fazackerley's skirt. He
had been feeling sick ever since they left the
main junction and climbed into the joggling, jolting
little train for the last lap of their journey, but the
sudden whistle had finished him.

Such a noise – it seemed to split the sky open.
'Enough to frighten the dead,' Miss Fazackerly said,
mopping her skirt and Nick's face with her handkerchief. He lay back limp as a rag and let her do it, the
way he always let people do things for him, not lifting
a finger. 'Poor lamb,' Miss Fazackerly said, but Carrie
looked stern.

'It's all his own fault. He's been stuffing his face ever since we left London. Greedy pig. *Dustbin.*'

He had not only eaten his own packed lunch – sandwiches and cold sausages and bananas – but most of Carrie's as well. She had let him have it to comfort him because he minded leaving home and their mother more than she did. Or had looked as if he minded more. She thought now that it was just one of his acts, put on to get sympathy. Sympathy and chocolate! He had had all her chocolate, too! 'I knew he'd be sick,' she said smugly.

'Might have warned me then, mightn't you?' Miss Fazackerly said. Not unkindly, she was one of the kindest teachers in the school, but Carrie wanted to cry suddenly. If she had been Nick she would have cried, or at least put on a hurt face. Being Carrie she stared crossly out of the carriage window at the big mountain on the far side of the valley. It was brown and purple on the top and green lower down; streaked with silver trickles of water and dotted with sheep.

Sheep and mountains. 'Oh, it'll be such fun,' their mother had said when she kissed them good-bye at the station. 'Living in the country instead of the stuffy old city. You'll love it, you see if you don't!' As if Hitler had arranged this old war for their benefit, just so that Carrie and Nick could be sent away in a train with gas masks slung over their shoulders and their names on cards round their necks. Labelled like parcels – Caroline Wendy Willow and Nicholas Peter Willow – only with no address to be sent to. None of them, not even the teachers, knew where they were going. 'That's part of the adventure,' Carrie's mother had said, and not just to cheer them up: it was her nature to look on the bright side. If she found herself in Hell, Carrie thought now, she'd just say, 'Well, at least we'll be *warm*.'

Thinking of her mother, always making the best of things (or pretending to: when the train began to move she had stopped smiling) Carrie nearly did cry. There was a lump like a pill stuck in her throat. She swallowed hard and pulled faces.

The train was slowing. 'Here we are,' Miss Fazackerly said. 'Collect your things, don't leave anything. Take care of Nick, Carrie.'

Carrie scowled. She loved Nick, loved him so much sometimes that it gave her a pain, but she hated to be told to do something she was going to do anyway. And she was bored with Nick at the moment. That dying-duck look as he struggled to get his case down from the rack! 'Leave it to me, silly baby,' she said, jumping up on the seat. Dust flew and he screwed up his face. 'You're making me sneeze,' he complained. 'Don't *bounce*, Carrie.'

They all seemed to have more luggage than when they had started. Suitcases that had once been quite light now felt as if they were weighed down with stones. And got heavier as they left the small station and straggled down a steep, cinder path. Carrie had Nick's case as well as her own and a carrier bag with a broken string handle. She tucked it under one arm, but it kept slipping backwards and her gas mask banged her knee as she walked.

'Someone help Caroline, please,' Miss Fazackerly cried, rushing up and down the line of children like a sheep dog. Someone did – Carrie felt the carrier bag go from under her arm, then one suitcase.

It was a bigger boy. Carrie blushed, but he wasn't a Senior: he wore a cap like all boys under sixteen, and although he was tall, he didn't look very much older than she was. She glanced sideways and said, 'Thank you *so* much,' in a grown-up voice like her mother's.

He grinned shyly back. He had steel-rimmed spectacles, a few spots on his chin. He said, 'Well, I suppose this is what they call our ultimate destination. Not much of a place, is it?'

They were off the cinder track now, walking down a hilly street where small, dark houses opened straight on to the pavement. There was sun on the mountain above them, but the town was in shadow; the air struck chill on their cheeks and smelled dusty.

'Bound to be dirty,' Carrie said. 'A coal-mining town.'

'I didn't mean dirt. Just that it's not big enough to have a good public library.'

It seemed a funny thing to bother about at the moment. Carrie said, 'The first place was bigger. Where we stopped at the junction.' She peered at his label and read his name. Albert Sandwich. She said, 'If you came earlier on in the alphabet you could have stayed there. You only just missed it, they divided us after the Rs. Do your friends call you Ally, or Bert?'

'I don't care for my name to be abbreviated,' he said.

'Nor do I like being called Jam, or Jelly, or even Peanut Butter.'

He spoke firmly but Carrie thought he looked anxious.

'I hadn't thought of sandwiches,' she said. 'Only of the town Sandwich in Kent, because my granny lives there. Though my dad says she'll have to move now in case the Germans land on the coast.' She thought of the Germans landing and her grandmother running away with her things on a cart like a refugee in a newspaper picture. She gave a loud, silly laugh and said, 'If they did, my gran 'ud give them What For. She's not frightened of anyone, I bet she could even stop Hitler. Go up on her roof and pour boiling oil down!'

Albert looked at her, frowning. 'I doubt if that would be very helpful. Old people aren't much use in a war. Like kids – best out of the way.'

His grave tone made Carrie feel foolish. She wanted to say it was only a joke, about boiling oil, but they had arrived at a building with several steps leading up and told to get into single file so that their names could be checked at the door. Nick was waiting there, holding Miss Fazackerly's hand. She said, 'There you are, darling. There she is, didn't I tell you?' And to Carrie, 'Don't lose him again!'

She ticked them off on her list, saying aloud, 'Two Willows, One Sandwich.'

Nick clung to Carrie's sleeve as they went through the door into a long, dark room with pointed windows.

It was crowded and noisy. Someone said to Carrie, 'Would you like a cup of tea, bach? And a bit of cake, now?' She was a cheerful, plump woman with a sing-song Welsh voice. Carrie shook her head; she felt cake would choke her. 'Stand by there, then,' the woman said. 'There by the wall with the others, and someone will choose you.'

Carrie looked round, bewildered, and saw Albert Sandwich. She whispered, 'What's happening?' and he said, 'A kind of cattle auction, it seems.'

He sounded calmly disgusted. He gave Carrie her suitcase, then marched to the end of the hall, sat down on his own, and took a book out of his pocket.

Carrie wished she could do that. Sit down and read as if nothing else mattered. But she had already begun to feel ill with shame at the fear that no one would choose her, the way she always felt when they picked teams at school. Suppose she was left to the last! She dragged Nick into the line of waiting children and stood, eyes on the ground, hardly daring to breathe. When someone called out, 'A nice little girl for Mrs Davies, now,' she felt she would suffocate. She looked up but unfocused her eyes so that passing faces blurred and swam in front of her.

Nick's hand tightened in hers. She looked at his white face and the traces of sick round his mouth and wanted to shake him. No one would take home a boy who looked like that, so pale and delicate. They would think he was bound to get ill and be a trouble to them. She said in a low, fierce voice, 'Why don't you smile and look nice,' and he blinked with surprise, looking so small and so sweet that she softened. She said, 'Oh, it's all right, I'm not cross. I won't leave you.'

Minutes passed, feeling like hours. Children left the line and were taken away. Only unwanted ones left, Carrie thought. She and Nick, and a few tough-looking boys, and an ugly girl with a squint who had two little sisters. And Albert Sandwich who was still sitting quietly on his suitcase, reading his book and taking no notice. *He* didn't care! Carrie tossed her head and hummed under her breath to show she didn't either.

Someone had stopped in front of her. Someone said, 'Surely you can take two, Miss Evans?'

'Two girls, perhaps. Not a boy and a girl, I'm afraid. I've only the one room, see, and my brother's particular.'

Particular about what, Carrie wondered. But Miss Evans looked nice; a little like a red squirrel Carrie had once seen, peering round a tree in a park. Reddish brown hair and bright, button eyes, and a shy, quivering look.

Carrie said, 'Nick sleeps in my room at home because he has bad dreams sometimes. I always look after him and he's no trouble at all.'

Miss Evans looked doubtful. 'Well, I don't know what my brother will say. Perhaps I can chance it.' She smiled at Carrie. 'There's pretty eyes you have, girl! Like green glass!'

Carrie smiled back. People didn't often notice her when Nick was around. *His* eyes were dark blue, like their mother's. She said, 'Oh, Nick's the pretty one, really.'

Miss Evans walked fast. She was a little woman, not much taller than Carrie, but she seemed as strong as a railway porter, carrying their cases as if they weighed nothing. Out of the hall down the street. They stopped outside a grocery shop with the name SAMUEL ISAAC EVANS above the door and Miss Evans took a key from her bag. She said, 'There's a back way and you'll use that, of course, but we'll go through the front for the once, as my brother's not here.'

The shop was dim and smelled mustily pleasant. Candles and tarred kindling, and spices, Carrie thought, wrinkling her nose. A door at the back led into a small room with a huge desk almost filling it. 'My brother's office,' Miss Evans said in a hushed voice and hurried them through into a narrow, dark hall with closed doors and a stair rising up. It was darker here than the shop and there was a strong smell of polish.

Polished linoleum, a shining, glass sea, with rugs scattered like islands. Not a speck of dust anywhere. Miss Evans looked down at their feet. 'Better change into your slippers before we go up to your bedroom.'

'We haven't got any,' Carrie said. She meant to explain that there hadn't been room in their cases but before she could speak Miss Evans turned bright red and said quickly, 'Oh, I'm so sorry, how silly of me, why should you? Never mind, as long as you're careful and tread on the drugget.'

A strip of white cloth covered the middle of the stair carpet. They trod on this as they climbed; looking back from the top, Carrie saw the marks of their rubber-soled shoes and felt guilty, though it wasn't her fault. Nick whispered, 'She thinks we're poor children, too poor to have slippers,' and giggled.

Carrie supposed he was right. Nick was good at guessing what people were thinking. But she didn't feel like giggling; everywhere was so tidy and clean it made her despair. She thought she would never dare touch anything in this house in case she left marks. She wouldn't dare *breathe* – even her breath might be dirty!

Miss Evans was looking at Nick. 'What did you say, dear?' she asked, but didn't wait for an answer. 'Here's the bathroom,' she said – proudly, it seemed. 'Hot and cold running water, *and* a flush toilet. And your room, just by here.'

It was a small room with two narrow beds and a hooked rug between them. A wardrobe and a wicker chair and a large, framed notice on the wall. The black letters said, The Eye Of The Lord Is Upon You.

Miss Evans saw Carrie looking at this. She said, 'My brother is very strong Chapel. So you'll have to be especially good, Sundays. No games or books, see? Except the Bible, of course.'

The children stared at her. She smiled shyly. 'It may not be what you're used to but it's better to get things straight from the start, isn't it? Mr Evans is a good man, but strict. Manners and tidiness and keeping things clean. He says dirt and sloppy habits are an insult to the Lord. So you will be good, won't you? You look like good children.'

It was almost as if she were pleading with them. Asking them to be good so that *she* wouldn't get into trouble. Carrie was sorry for her, though she felt very uncomfortable. Neither she nor Nick were particularly tidy; at home, in their warm, muddly house, no one had expected them to be. Milly, their maid, always picked up their toys and made their beds and put their clothes away. Carrie said, 'We'll try to be good, Miss Evans.'

'Call me Auntie,' Miss Evans said. 'Auntie Louise. Or Auntie Lou, if that's easier. But you'd best call my brother Mr Evans. You see, he's a Councillor.' She paused and then went on in the same proud tone she had used when she showed them the bathroom, 'Mr Evans is a very important man. He's at a Council meeting just now. I think I'd best give you your supper before he comes back, hadn't I?'

They had a good supper of eggs and milk and crunchy, fresh bread in the kitchen which was as clean as the rest of the house but more cheerful with a big range fire that threw out heat like a furnace. Miss Evans didn't eat with them but stood by the table like a waitress in a restaurant, taking the plates to the sink as soon as they'd cleared them and sweeping up crumbs round their chairs before they had finished drinking their milk. She didn't actually say, 'Please hurry up, oh, *please* hurry up,' but she might just as well have done:

her mouth twitched as if she were muttering it inwardly, her eyes kept darting to the clock on the mantelpiece and there were red, nervous spots on her cheeks.

She made the children nervous too. When she said, 'What about bed, now?' they were more than glad to escape from the kitchen where the Very Important Councillor Evans might appear any minute. As they went upstairs, Miss Evans rolled up the drugget behind them. 'Mr Evans doesn't like to see it down,' she explained when she caught Carrie's eye. 'I just put it there while he's out to keep the carpet spick and span. It's a new one, you see, lovely deep pile, and Mr Evans doesn't want it trodden on.'

'How are you supposed to get up the stairs, then?' Nick said. 'Walk on the ceiling, or fly like a bird?'

'Well. Well, of course . . .' Miss Evans laughed, rather breathlessly. 'Of course you have to walk on it sometimes but not too often. Mr Evans said twice a day would be quite enough. You see, four of us going up and down twice a day, morning and evening, makes *sixteen* times altogether, and Mr Evans thinks that's quite enough traipsing. So if you could try to remember to bring down all the things you'll want for the day, in the morning . . .'

'But the *bathroom's* upstairs,' Nick said in an outraged voice.

She looked at him apologetically. 'Yes, I know, dear. But if you want to – you know – *go anywhere*, there's one at the end of the yard. Mr Evans doesn't use it, of course, it wouldn't be dignified for him to be seen going there, not a man in his position, when all the neighbours know he's got one indoors, but *I* use it, and though it's an earth closet it's quite nice and clean.'

Nick stared as if he couldn't believe his ears. Carrie nudged him gently and said, 'That'll be fun, Nick, won't it? Like the one at that farm where we stayed last summer.'

'Spiders.' Nick's eyes rounded with remembered horror. 'There was *spiders*!'

'God's Creatures,' Miss Evans said. 'Just like you, dear.'

'Not like me. Not like me *at all*!' Nick's voice rose in a loud, breathy cry. 'I don't have hundreds and hundreds of creepy-crawly legs and I don't eat flies for my dinner or spin sticky stuff out of my tummy. That's disgusting, spiders is disgusting, horrible and *yakky* and disgusting . . .'

'Bathroom for you,' Carrie said, marching him in. 'If you don't shut up *now*, I'll squeeze a cold flannel right down the back of your neck.'

She had closed the door. When Nick was quiet, which was almost at once (cold water was almost as hateful as spiders) Miss Evans whispered timidly through it, 'Do be quick, dear, time's getting on . . .'

They couldn't be very quick because there was no electric light upstairs and they had to manage with the candle Carrie was holding. She couldn't find Nick's face flannel by its flickering light and he wouldn't use hers. And their mother had screwed up the tube of toothpaste so tightly that the lid wouldn't budge.

'Have to go without cleaning your teeth just for once,' Carrie said.

'I *won't*. My mouth feels all furry and yakky. Horrible, Carrie. Beastly and horrible and disgusting . . .'

A door banged downstairs and stopped him mid-wail, mouth hanging open. He looked at Carrie with eyes like black pits. 'Oh,' he said, '*Carrie* . . .'

Her own heart was thumping, banging about in her chest like a tennis ball. 'Come on,' she said, and whisked him out of the bathroom.

Miss Evans as standing outside. 'Into bed now,' she said softly, hustling them past here. Then began scuttering backwards and forwards like a small, frightened mouse, picking up the things they had dropped, clothes in the bedroom, toothpaste tube in the bathroom. 'Oh dear,' she was saying, under her breath, 'oh dear, oh dear, oh dear . . .'

'Lou,' a man's voice shouted. 'Lou! What are you up to?'

'Coming, Samuel,' Miss Evans called from the landing. 'Just a minute.'

'What are you doing up there? I might have known, I suppose. Up and down the stairs, soon as my back's turned, wearing out the stair carpet . . .'

Safe in bed, Carrie blew out the candle. Miss Evans shut the door. The loud, hectoring voice went on. 'Messing and humbugging about, up and down, back and for, in and out, messing and humbugging about . . .'

It was velvet dark in the room, no light from the

window because the thick, blackout curtains were drawn. They lay quite still in the darkness, listening to the roar of Mr Evans's voice and the thin squeak of his sister's. Like a mouse answering a lion, Carrie thought. Then the heavy tread of feet down the passage. The bang of another door. And silence at last.

For several minutes neither of them dared to break it. Then Nick said, 'I want Mummy.'

Carrie got out of her bed and felt her way into his. He clutched at her and wound himself round her like an octopus, or like ivy, his cold feet in her stomach. 'I want to go home,' he said. 'I don't like it here. I don't want to be safe in the country. I want Mummy and Milly and Dad.'

'You've got me,' Carrie held him tight to comfort them both. She said, 'It won't seem so bad in the morning.'

He was shaking and shivering. He whispered into her ear, 'He must be an Ogre, Carrie. A horrible, disgusting, real-life OGRE.'

He wasn't an Ogre, of course. Just a tall, thin, cross man with a loud voice, pale, staring, pop-eyes, and tufts of spiky hair sticking out from each nostril.

Councillor Samuel Isaac Evans was a bully. He bullied his sister. He even bullied the women who came into his shop, selling them things they didn't really want to buy and refusing to stock things that they did. 'Take it or leave it,' he'd say. 'Don't you know there's a war on?'

He would have bullied the children if he had thought they were frightened of him. But although Carrie was a little frightened, she didn't show it, and Nick wasn't frightened at all. He was frightened of Ogres and spiders and crabs and cold water and the dentist and dark nights, but he wasn't often frightened of people. Perhaps this was only because he had never had reason to be until he met Mr Evans, but he wasn't afraid of him, even after that first, dreadful night, because Mr Evans had false teeth that clicked when he talked. 'You can't really be scared of someone whose teeth might fall out,' he told Carrie.

The possibility fascinated him from the beginning, from the moment Mr Evans walked into the kitchen while they were having breakfast their first morning and bared those loose teeth in what he probably thought was a smile. It looked to the children more like the kind of grin a tiger might give before it pounced on its prey. They put down their porridge spoons and stood up, politely and meekly.

It seemed to please him. He said, 'You've got a few manners, I see. That's something! That's a bit of sugar on the pill!'

They didn't know what to say to this so they said nothing and he stood there, grinning and rubbing his hands together. At last he said, 'Sit down, then, finish your breakfast, what are you waiting for? It's a wicked Sin to let good food get cold. You've fallen on your feet, let me tell you, you'll get good food in this house. So no faddiness mind! No whining round my sister for titbits when my back's turned. Particularly the boy. I know what boys are! Walking stomachs! I told her, you fetch two girls now, there's just the one room, but she got round me, she said, the boy's only a babby!' He looked sharply at Nick. 'Not too much of a babby, I hope. No wet beds. That I won't stand!'

Nick's gaze was fixed on Mr Evans's mouth. 'That's a rude thing to mention,' he said in a clear, icy voice that made Carrie tremble. But Mr Evans didn't fly into the rage she'd expected. He simply looked startled – as if a worm had just lifted its head and answered him back, Carrie thought.

He sucked his teeth for a minute. Then said, surprisingly mildly, 'All right. All right, then. You mind your Ps and Qs, see, and I won't complain. As long as you toe the chalk line! Rules are made to be kept in this house, no shouting, or running upstairs, and no Language.' Nick looked at him and he went on – quickly, as if he knew what was coming, 'No *Bad* Language, that is, I'll have no foul mouths here. I don't know how you've been brought up but this house is run in the Fear of the Lord.'

Nick said, 'We don't swear. Even my father doesn't swear. And he's a Naval Officer.'

What an odd thing to say, Carrie thought. But Mr Evans was looking at Nick with a certain, grudging respect.

'Oh, an Officer, is he? Well, well.'

'A Captain,' Nick said. 'Captain Peter Willow.'

'Indeed?' Mr Evans's teeth clicked – to attention, perhaps. He said, grinning again, 'Then let's hope he's taught you how to behave. It'll save me the trouble,' and turned on his heel and went back to the shop.

Silence fell. Miss Evans moved from the sink where she'd been all this time, standing quite still, and started to clear the plates from the table.

Nick said, 'You don't mind Language, do you? I mean, I don't know the deaf and dumb alphabet.'

'Don't be smart,' Carrie said, but Miss Evans laughed. Hand to her mouth, bright squirrel eyes watching the door as if she were scared he'd come back and catch her.

She said softly, 'Oh, his bark's worse than his bite. Though he won't stand to be crossed, so don't be too cheeky and mind what he says! *I've* always minded him – he's so much older, you see. When our mam died – our dad had been killed down the pit long before – he took me in and brought me up. His wife was alive then, poor, dear soul, and his son's not much younger than I am. That's Frederick, he's away in the Army. Mr Evans brought us up together, made no difference between us. Never made me feel my place. When we were naughty he'd give Fred the strap but he'd sit me on the mantelpiece to make me mind my manners. I've sat there many a time, scared to death of the fire and my feet pins and needles.'

She looked at the mantelpiece above the range fire and the children looked at it too. It was a horribly long way from the ground. Miss Evans said, 'You might say he's been more like a father to me than a brother.'

'Our father never sat anyone on a mantelpiece,' Nick said. 'Or frightened anyone.'

★

Carrie wasn't really much afraid of Mr Evans. But she kept out of his way as his sister's scraggy old cat did, streaking from its place by the fire the moment his feet were heard in the passage. Not that he had ever kicked the cat, Carrie thought; it was just wary, as she was. 'Animals know,' she said to Nick, 'when people aren't friendly.'

Though perhaps in his blustery way he did try to be friends with them. He never shared their meals, eating by himself in the parlour with Miss Evans waiting on him, but sometimes he would come into the kitchen while they were having their tea and say, 'Well, Caroline, it's a fine day for the race, isn't it?' 'What race?' she would ask, as she was expected to, and he would answer, 'The Human Race,' and nearly lose his teeth laughing.

And he let them help in the shop (Carrie loved that: measuring out things on the scales and giving the change) until Nick stole some biscuits one day and he came in and caught him.

They had been there three weeks. Miss Evans had become Auntie Lou and it seemed they had known her for ever. It was about six o'clock and Carrie was helping to wash up the tea things when she heard Mr Evans's bellow of rage.

She ran into the shop. Nick was standing there, white as flour, with ginger biscuit crumbs round his mouth, and Mr Evans was shouting.

'Thief! Caught red-handed now, aren't you? How long has this been going on? Sneaking in here when the shop's closed and I'm safely out of the way in the parlour? Stealing! The ingratitude of it! Oh, you'll be sorry, you'll pay. You need a sharp lesson, my lad, and I don't mind giving it. Strap's what you're asking for, isn't it?' He began to unbuckle his belt. He said, gloatingly, 'On your bare bottom!'

Carrie gasped. Nick had never been beaten, not even a slap! He was standing there, shivering! What could she do? Fetch the police? But Nick had been *stealing*! Auntie Lou? *She* was no use – she'd not even come to see what was happening. She was probably standing in the kitchen, listening and wringing her hands . . .

She said, 'Please, Mr Evans. Oh, please. He's only a little boy. Not a thief, just a little boy who likes biscuits. He's got an awful sweet tooth, he can't help it. I don't suppose he thought it was stealing.'

'Then he'll have to learn to think, won't he?' Mr Evans said.

He advanced on Nick who had retreated as far as he could. Was standing with his back to the shop door and staring. He said, 'If you hit me, I'll tell. I'll go to school and tell my teacher.'

Mr Evans laughed. 'And what will she say, my young master? That it's a fine thing you've done, to steal from the good people who have taken you in?'

'I'll say I was hungry,' Nick said.

Mr Evans stopped moving. Carrie couldn't see his face because she was behind him but she could see Nick's. He was so pale she thought he would faint, but his eyes were dark and steady.

A hundred years seemed to pass. They all stood quite still, as if frozen. Then, very slowly, Mr Evans fastened his belt round his trousers . . .

He prayed for Nick that night. On his knees, by the bed, Nick kneeling beside him.

'O Lord, look down upon this sinful child in his wickedness and lead him from his evil ways into right-eousness. If he is tempted again, remind him of the pains of Thy Hell, the torment and burning, so that he may quiver in his wretched flesh and repent in his immortal soul . . .'

He prayed for about half an hour. Carrie thought she would rather have been beaten, herself, but Nick was triumphant. 'I knew I could stop him if I said I was hungry,' he said when it was all over. 'Grown-ups don't mind being nasty to children but they don't like other grown-ups to *know* they've been nasty.'

He sounded smugly cheerful but Carrie was nervous. She felt Nick had made an enemy of Mr Evans and that might turn out to be dangerous.

'He's not so nasty really,' she said. 'You shouldn't have pinched his biscuits, you know you shouldn't, you're not such a baby. And it was mean to say you were hungry because it's simply not true, you're just greedy for biscuits. And I know he's nasty to Auntie Lou sometimes but it's her own fault because she lets him be. She's nice, Auntie Lou, but she's stupid.'

'It isn't her fault, he *is* nasty,' Nick said. 'He's *mean* nasty. You know he yelled at Auntie Lou yesterday because he slipped on the mat in the hall? He said she'd polished underneath it but she hadn't. I was standing in the kitchen, he didn't see me but I saw *him*. I saw him move the mat so it should be on a slippery bit, and then sort of pretend to slip *on* it, and then start to shout.' He stopped. They were in the same bed. He put his hand into Carrie's. It felt small and boneless. 'I hate him,' he said with a shake in his voice, 'I really and truly do hate him.'

Carrie said slowly, 'If you really do hate it here, then we ought to tell someone.' But her heart sank. Who could she tell? Their mother and father were so far away and you couldn't write that sort of thing in a letter. Miss Fazackerly? She had said, 'Come and tell me if things aren't all right in your billets.' But what could she do, if they did? There were so many evacuees in the town and not enough places to stay, so the teachers said. The houses were small and some of the children were having to sleep three to a bed. How could she go to Miss Fazackerly and say, 'I'm sorry but we don't want to stay with Mr Evans any more because he caught Nick stealing his biscuits?'

'Oh, I don't hate being here,' Nick said, sounding surprised. 'I just hate *him*, that's all. But I don't want to *leave*, I'm used to it now.'

It seemed, in fact, as if they had lived there all their lives long. Slept in that bedroom, eaten in that kitchen; used the earth privy in the daytime (Nick got constipated because of the spiders); kept out of Mr Evans's way; woken up to the pit hooter wailing; gone running to school down the hilly, main street . . .

Nick went to the local Primary because he was still young enough but the older children were given lessons by their own teachers in the Chapels. Ebenezer Chapel, Siloa Chapel – cold, gloomy places with pictures of dead, bearded Chapel Elders looking down from the walls. It was quite different from going to school in London. More *fun*, Carrie thought, and was glad she hadn't been left behind, as some of her friends had been, in the big town at the other end of the valley. There was a new Secondary there, a fine building everyone said, with playing fields and a pool and modern laboratories but it sounded, to Carrie, very ordinary and dull. She missed her friends but she didn't envy them – though she thought Albert Sandwich probably did: he was the sort of boy who would prefer to be taught in a proper school. She looked for him once or twice; even went one day to the tiny public library which was in a room with stained glass windows at the back of the Town Hall, but she couldn't find him. Perhaps he had got himself moved to the bigger town, or perhaps he had gone home to London as some of the children had done. The unhappy ones who were homesick for their mothers.

Carrie's mother wasn't in London any more. Her father's ship was on convoy duty in the North Sea, and her mother had gone to live in Glasgow so she could see him when he came into port. She wrote to Carrie and Nick and said she was living in a boarding house in a street near the docks, in a dark little room that smelt of kippers. She said how glad she was they had somewhere nice to stay and that she hoped they were being good and making their beds and helping with the washing up and remembering to clean their teeth. She said she was driving an ambulance in the air raids and that it was very exciting but dreadfully tiring; sometimes she went to bed after breakfast and slept until evening. She sent them sweets sometimes, and several pairs of red socks she had knitted while she was waiting for a call at the ambulance station, and a photograph of herself in her uniform with a tin hat on. They showed this to Auntie Lou and she gave them a frame so that they could hang it in their bedroom, but they didn't look at it much. It was a good likeness of their mother and she was smiling at them but she didn't belong in the Evanses' house. Like their father, and Milly their help, who was working in a munitions factory, and Bongo their dog (their mother hadn't said what had happened to *him*) she belonged somewhere else. Somewhere far away and long ago. In a dream, in another life . . .

The summer ended. Autumn came and they picked bilberries on the mountain: tiny, purple fruit that stained their teeth and their clothes. Autumn became winter and it turned steely cold. A feathery pattern of ice covered the mud of the yard and cracked under their feet as they ran to the privy, and it wasn't much warmer indoors. When they went into their bedroom at night, cold air came up from the polished linoleum like air off an ice rink. The only comfortable place was the kitchen; they toasted their raw hands and feet by the fire and the heat made their chilblains itch.

'You've got chilblains!' their mother said when she came to see them at the beginning of December. She had travelled overnight all the way from Scotland, just for a few hours one Saturday. They had looked forward to seeing her but when she came they didn't know what to say. She had had her hair cut. She looked different with her hair cut and it made them feel shy. Or perhaps they felt shy anyway, seeing her here where she didn't belong. They put their hands behind their backs and said, 'Oh, we've all got chilblains at school.'

They had lunch in the parlour, a dreary room with slippery, brown leather chairs, a harmonium against one wall, and a case of dead, stuffed birds hanging on another. Mr Evans closed the shop for an extra half hour and brought out a bottle of sherry. He didn't drink himself but he poured a glass for their mother and was really quite jolly. He even patted Nick on the head and called him 'Young Nicodemus', which amazed Nick so much he sat with his mouth hanging open and barely touched the roast meat on his plate. That was a pity, Carrie thought. They didn't often get roast meat, only what Auntie Lou called 'Done Down', which was the remains of the joint after Mr Evans had finished with it, minced up with bread and gravy browning. 'Young people shouldn't have meat, it makes them too boisterous,' was what Mr Evans said.

But today he cut them each two thick slices, beautifully juicy with blood. He said to their mother, 'They
eat like troopers, you don't have to worry. Not that
we have more than our ration, you know, in spite of
the shop! No easy come, easy go, in this house! I was
brought up in a hard school, Mrs Willow, and I don't
forget it. Children today don't know that they're born.
Not that I've any complaints about your two, don't
mistake me. I don't stand any nonsense, mind you,
they do what I tell them and they speak when they're
spoken to, but they know where they are with me.
Don't you, young Nick?'

Young Nick said nothing.

Carrie said, 'Yes, we do, Mr Evans.'

They had rice pudding and jam after the beef. Then
Auntie Lou made tea and put the biscuit barrel on the
table. Nick shook his head when it was offered to him.
'But you like biscuits, darling,' his mother said. Nick
stared and said nothing.

Auntie Lou didn't speak either. She was like a ghost
at the table, a shy shadow, watching her brother and
pleating her apron with nervous, red fingers. But when
it was time for the children to take their mother to the
station, she drew a deep breath and said, 'I do my best
for them, Mrs Willow. I do really.'

Their mother looked surprised. Then she kissed
Auntie Lou on the cheek and said, 'Thank you, oh, I *do*
thank you,' and Auntie Lou smiled and blushed as if
she had been given a present.

When they first left the house, none of them spoke

for a while. Carrie was frightened, she didn't know why.

Then their mother said, 'It's rather cold in your bedroom.' It wasn't a question but it sounded like one.

Nick didn't answer. He was stumping along, looking straight ahead and frowning.

'Oh, we don't mind that,' Carrie said. 'We're not *nesh*.'

'What's *nesh*?' their mother asked.

'A Welsh word for feeble.'

'Oh! Oh, I see.'

Their mother gave a queer laugh. Almost a shy sort of laugh, Carrie thought, though it couldn't be. Their mother was never shy. 'I expect it's a bit strange,' she said, 'all that Chapel and being seen and not heard. But it's an experience, isn't it? Not like being at home of course, not so cosy, but I expect it's quite interesting. And they seem very kind in their way. Doing their best for you.'

Nick still said nothing. His silence frightened Carrie and she knew why, suddenly. She was afraid that any minute now he could come out with it, that he'd say he hated Mr Evans and not being allowed to use the bathroom in the daytime, even when it was cold. That he hated the cold and his chilblains and the earth privy and the spiders and not being allowed to eat biscuits and only having roast beef for dinner because *she* had come. Carrie would have died rather than say these things but Nick wouldn't be embarrassed: he could say them without turning a hair! And if he did, it would upset their mother – though thinking about it, Carrie thought she didn't mind that too much. What she did mind – minded quite horribly – was that it would upset Auntie Lou. *Her poor face at dinner*, she thought. *Her poor face . . .*

But all Nick said was, 'Mr Evans cheats when he counts saccharine tablets.'

Their mother laughed. She sounded relieved as if she, like Carrie, had been afraid to hear something worse. She said, 'Oh, my lamb, what do you mean?'

Carrie said, 'He sells saccharines in packets because of the sugar ration. We count them out for him sometimes. I quite like doing it because of the funny taste on my fingers. But there ought to be a hundred in each packet and Nick once counted a packet that *he'd* done – Mr Evans, I mean – over again, and there were only ninety-seven. But Mr Evans just made a mistake, he isn't dishonest.'

Their mother laughed again. Laughed and laughed like a little girl laughing. She said, 'Well, if that's the worst thing . . .'

And after that she seemed happy the rest of the way, saying how lovely it had been to see them even for such a short time and how she'd come down again when she could, but it was such a long way and the trains were so crowded with soldiers and she had had to take two whole days off from the ambulance station. She couldn't do that again for a while, she had to be on duty over Christmas as it was. And though that would be a sad time for her, in Glasgow, alone, it would cheer her up to think what fun *they* were having! Christmas in a wild Welsh valley with the stars shining on top of the mountains and everyone singing and singing, the way they all sang in Wales; so beautifully, natural as birds!

She said, 'I expect it'll be something you'll remember and treasure for the rest of your lives,' and Carrie was pleased because she sounded like herself for the first time that day.

Only at the last minute, at the station, did she seem sad again. Leaning out of the window, just before the guard blew his whistle, she said in a desperate voice, 'My darlings, my darlings, you are happy here, aren't you?' and Carrie was more than frightened then; she was terrified. Terrified that Nick would say no, he wasn't happy at all, and that their mother would get out of the train and go back to the house and pack their things and take them away. After poor Auntie Lou had tried so hard to be nice!

But Nick looked gravely at their mother and then smiled, very sweetly, and said, 'Oh, I like it here very much. I don't ever want to go home again. I simply *love* Auntie Lou. She's the nicest person I've ever met in my whole life.'

Nick had been born a week before Christmas. On his birthday Auntie Lou gave him a pair of leather gloves with fur linings and Mr Evans gave him a Holy Bible with a soft, red cover and pictures inside.

Nick said, 'Thank you, Mr Evans,' very politely, but without smiling. Then he put the Bible down and said, 'Auntie Lou, what *lovely* gloves, they're the best gloves I've ever had in my whole life. I'll keep them for ever and ever, even when I've grown too big for them. My tenth birthday gloves!'

Carrie felt sorry for Mr Evans. She said, 'The Bible's lovely too, you are lucky, Nick.' And later, when she and Nick were alone, 'It was kind of him, really. I expect when he was a little boy he'd rather have had a Bible for his birthday than anything else in the world, even a bicycle. So it was kind of him to think you might feel like that, too.'

'But I didn't want a Bible,' Nick said. 'I'd rather have had a knife. He's got some smashing knives in the shop on a card by the door. A Special Offer. I've been looking at them every day and hoping I'd get one and he knew that's what I was hoping. I looked at them and he saw me looking. It was just mean of him to give me a rotten old Bible instead.'

'Perhaps he'll give you a knife for Christmas,' Carrie said, though she doubted it, in her heart. If Mr Evans really knew Nick wanted a knife, he was unlikely to give him one. He thought it was bad for people to get what they wanted. 'Want must be your master,' was what he always said.

Carrie sighed. She didn't like Mr Evans, no one could, but Nick hating him so much made her dislike him less. 'He's getting us a goose for Christmas,' she said, 'that'll be nice, won't it? I've never had a goose.'

'I'd rather have a turkey!' Nick said.

The goose was to come from Mr Evans's older sister who lived outside the town and kept poultry. Nick and Carrie had never heard of her until now. 'She's a bit of an invalid,' Auntie Lou said. 'Bed-fast much of the time now. Poor soul, I think of her but I daren't go to see her. Mr Evans won't have it. Dilys has made her bed and turned her back on her own people, is what he says, and that's that. She married Mr Gotobed, the mine-owner, you see.'

The children didn't see but didn't like to ask. It made Auntie Lou nervous to be asked direct questions. So they said, 'Gotobed's a funny name, isn't it?'

'English, of course,' Auntie Lou said. 'That upset Mr Evans to start with! An Englishman *and* a mine-owner, too! She married him just after our dad was killed down the pit – dancing on our father's grave, was what Mr Evans called it. The Gotobeds were bad owners, you see; our dad was killed by a rock fall that would never have happened, Mr Evans says, if they'd taken proper safety precautions. Not that it was young Mr Gotobed's fault, *his* father was alive then, and in charge of the mine, but Mr Evans says all that family is tarred with the same brush, only thinking of profits. So it made him hard against Dilys. Even now her husband's dead, he's not willing to let bygones be bygones.'

Though he was willing to accept a goose at Christmas, apparently. 'They're always fine birds,' Auntie Lou said – as if this was sufficient reason. 'Hepzibah Green rears them. She's good with poultry. Fine, light hand with pastry, too. You should taste her mince pies! Hepzibah looks after Dilys *and* the place best she can. Druid's Bottom was a fine house once, though it's run down since Mr Gotobed passed on and Dilys took bad. Needs a man's eye, Mr Evans says, though he's not willing to give it, and Dilys won't ask, of course.' She sighed gently. 'They're both proud people, see?'

'Druid's *Bottom*,' Nick said, and giggled.

'Bottom of Druid's Grove,' Auntie Lou said. 'That's the cwm where the yew trees grow. Do you remember where we picked those blackberries up by the railway line? The deep cwm, just before the tunnel?'

Nick's eyes widened. He said, '*That dark place!*'

'It's the yews make it dark,' Auntie Lou said. 'Though it's a queer place, too. Full of the old religion still, people say – not a place to go after dark. Not alone, anyway. I know I'd not care to, though I wouldn't let Mr Evans hear me say it. Wicked foolishness, he calls that sort of talk. There's nothing to be afraid of on this earth he says, not for those who trust in the Lord.'

Carrie was excited; she loved old, spooky tales. 'I wouldn't be afraid of the Grove,' she boasted. 'Nick might be, he's a *baby*, but I'm not scared of anything. Can I come with you, Auntie Lou, when you go to fetch the goose?'

But as it turned out, she and Nick went alone. On what was, perhaps, the most important journey they ever made together.

They were due to go to Druid's Bottom two days before Christmas, but Auntie Lou was ill. She coughed all morning and her eyes were red-rimmed. After midday dinner, Mr Evans came into the kitchen and looked at her, coughing over the sink. 'You're not fit to go out,' he said. 'Send the children.'

Auntie Lou coughed and coughed. 'I thought I'd go

tomorrow instead. Hepzibah will know I'm not coming now it's getting so late. I'll be better tomorrow.'

'I'll want you in the shop, Christmas Eve,' Mr Evans said. 'The children can go. Earn their keep for a change.'

'It'll be a heavy goose, Samuel.'

'They can manage between them.'

There was a short silence. Auntie Lou avoided the children's eyes. Then she said, uneasily, 'It'll be dark before they get back.'

'Full moon,' Mr Evans said. He looked at the children, at Nick's horrified face, and then at Auntie Lou. She began to blush painfully. He said in a quiet and ominous voice, 'You've not been putting ideas in their heads, I do hope!'

Auntie Lou looked at the children, too. Her expression begged them not to give her away. Carrie felt impatient with her – no grown-up should be so weak and so silly – but she was sorry as well. She said innocently, 'What ideas, Mr Evans? Of course we'd love to go, we don't mind the dark.'

'There's nothing *to* mind,' she said to Nick as they trudged along the railway line. 'What is there to be scared of? Just a few old trees.'

Nick said nothing; only sighed.

Carrie said, 'All that queer place stuff is just Auntie Lou being superstitious. You know how superstitious she is, touching wood and not walking under ladders and throwing salt over her shoulder when she's spilled some. I'm not surprised Mr Evans gets cross with her sometimes. She's so scared, she'd jump at her own shadow.'

But when they reached the Grove, Carrie felt a little less bold. It was growing dusk; stars were pricking out in the cold sky above them. And it was so quiet, suddenly, that their ears seemed to be singing.

Carrie whispered, 'There's the path down. By that stone.'

Nick's pale face glimmered as he looked up at her. He whispered back, 'You go. I'll wait here.'

'Don't be silly.' Carrie swallowed – then pleaded with him. 'Don't you want a nice mince pie? We might get a mince pie. And it's not far. Auntie Lou said it wasn't far down the hill. Not much more than five minutes.'

Nick shook his head. He screwed up his eyes and put his hands over his ears.

Carrie said coldly, 'All right, have it your own way. But it'll be dark soon and you'll be really scared then. Much more scared by yourself than you would be with me. Druids and ghosts coming to get you! Wild animals too – you don't *know*! I wouldn't be surprised if there were wolves in these mountains. But *I* don't care. Even if I hear them howling and snapping their jaws I shan't hurry.'

And she marched off without looking back. White stones marked the path through the yew trees and in the steep places there were steps cut in the earth and shored up with wood. She hadn't gone far when she heard Nick wailing behind her, 'Carrie, wait for me, *wait* . . .' She stopped and he skidded into her back. 'Don't leave me, Carrie!'

'I thought it was you leaving *me*,' she said, making a joke of it, to comfort him, and he tried to laugh but it turned into a sob in his throat.

He hung on to the back of her coat, whimpering under his breath as she led the way down the path. The yew trees grew densely, some of them covered with ivy that rustled and rattled. Like scales, Carrie thought; the trees were like live creatures with scales. She told herself not to be stupid, but stopped to draw breath. She said, 'Do be quiet, Nick.'

'Why?'

'I don't know,' Carrie said. 'Something . . .'

She couldn't explain it. It was such a strange feeling. As if there was something here, something *waiting*. Deep in the trees or deep in the earth. Not a ghost – nothing so simple. Whatever it was had no name. Something old and huge and nameless, Carrie thought, and started to tremble.

Nick said, 'Carrie . . .'

'Listen.'

'What for?'

'*Sssh* . . .'

No sound at first. Then she heard it. A kind of slow, dry whisper, or sigh. As if the earth were turning in its sleep. Or the huge, nameless thing were breathing.

'Did you hear?' Carrie said. 'Did you *hear*?'

Nick began to cry piteously. Silence now, except for his weeping.

Carrie said, dry-mouthed, 'It's gone now. It wasn't anything. There's nothing there, really.'

Nick gulped, trying hard to stop crying. Then he clutched Carrie. 'Yes there is! There is *now*!'

Carrie listened. It wasn't the sound she had heard before but something quite different. A queer, throaty, chuckling, gobbling sound that seemed to come from somewhere above them, higher up the path. They stood still as stone. The sound was coming closer.

'*Run*,' Carrie said. She began to run, stumbling. The big bag they had brought for the goose caught between her legs and almost threw her down but she recovered her balance, her feet slipping and sliding. She ran, and Nick ran behind her, and the creature, whatever it was, the gobbling *Thing*, followed them. It seemed to be calling to them and Carrie thought of fairy tales she had read – you looked back at something behind you and were caught in its spell! She gasped, 'Don't look back, Nick, whatever you do.'

The path widened and flattened as it came out of the Grove and she caught Nick's hand to make him run faster. Too fast for his shorter legs and he fell on his knees. He moaned, as she pulled him up, 'I can't, I *can't*, Carrie . . .'

She said, through chattering teeth, 'Yes, you *can*. Not much farther.'

They saw the house then, its dark, tall-chimneyed bulk looming up, and lights in the windows. One light quite high up and one low down, at the side. They ran, on rubbery legs, through an open gate and across a dirt yard towards the lit window. There was a door but it was shut. They flung themselves against it.

Gobble-Gobble was coming behind them, was crossing the yard.

'Please,' Carrie croaked. 'Please.' Quite sure that it was too late, that the creature would get them.

But the door opened inward, like magic, and they fell through it to light, warmth, and safety.

CHAPTER 5

A warm, safe, lighted place.

Hepzibah's kitchen was always like that, and not only that evening. Coming into it was like coming home on a bitter cold day to a bright, leaping fire. It was like the smell of bacon when you were hungry; loving arms when you were lonely; safety when you were scared . . .

Not that they stopped being scared at once, that first, frightened time. They were indoors, it was true, but the door was still open. And the woman seemed in no hurry to close it and shut out the dangerous night; she simply stood, looking down at the children and smiling.

She was tall with shining hair the colour of copper. She wore a white apron, the sleeves of her dress were rolled up, showing big, fair, freckled arms, and there was flour on her hands.

Carrie saw her, then the room. A big, stone-flagged kitchen, shadowy in the corners but bright near the fire. A dresser with blue and white plates; a scrubbed, wooden table; a hanging oil lamp. And Albert Sandwich, sitting at the table with an open book where the light fell upon it.

He opened his mouth to speak but Carrie had turned. She said, 'Shut the door!' The woman looked puzzled – people were always so *slow*, Carrie thought. She said desperately, 'Miss Evans sent us for the goose. But something chased us. We ran and ran but it chased us. Sort of *gobbling*.'

The woman peered where she pointed, out into the night.

'Oh, shut the *door*,' Carrie cried. 'It'll come *in*.'

The woman smiled broadly. She had lovely, white teeth with a gap in the middle. 'Bless you, love, it's only Mister Johnny. I didn't know he was out.'

'He went to shut up the chickens,' Albert Sandwich said. 'I expect he went for a walk after.'

'But it wasn't a *person*,' Carrie said, speaking slowly to make them understand. She wasn't so frightened now. Albert had spoken so calmly that it made her calm too. She said, 'It didn't talk, it went *gobble-gobble*.'

'That's Mister Johnny's way of talking,' Albert Sandwich said. 'You must admit, Hepzibah, it could frighten someone.' He looked at Carrie, quite sternly. 'Though I expect you frightened him just as much. How would you feel if people ran away from you when you didn't mean to hurt them?'

Hepzibah called softly into the darkness, 'It's all right, Mister Johnny, all right, come on in.' Her voice wasn't Welsh. A different, throatier, accent.

Someone appeared in the doorway and stood close to Hepzibah, as if for protection. A small person in a tweed suit and a spotted bow tie with a shy, scrumpled-up face. He tried to smile but he couldn't smile properly: one side of his mouth seemed dragged down.

Hepzibah said, 'This is Mister Johnny Gotobed, children. Mister Johnny, say how-do-you-do to our visitors, will you?'

He looked at her and made that queer sound in his throat. Chuckle-gobble – only now it did seem like talking. Some strange, unknown language. He rubbed his right hand on his trousers and looked at it. Then held it out, shakily.

Carrie couldn't move. Though he wasn't a ghost she was still too scared to touch that small, shaky hand. But Nick said, 'Hallo, Mister Johnny,' and went up to him as if it were the easiest and most natural thing in the world. 'I'm Nick,' he said. 'Nicholas Peter Willow and I'm just ten. It was my birthday last week. And Carrie, my sister, will be twelve next May.'

'Hch. Harch-a. Chala. Larschla,' Mister Johnny said. He spat a bit as he spoke and Carrie dreaded the moment when she would have to shake hands and be spat at.

But Hepzibah saved her. She said, 'The goose is ready for you. But you'll take a little something first, won't you? Albert, take Carrie to fetch the goose while I set the table.'

Albert took a candle from the dresser and lit it. Carrie followed him, through a door at the back of the kitchen, down a stone passage into a dairy. The goose lay, neatly trussed, on a cold, marble slab. There were speckly eggs in trays on the shelf, slabs of pale, oozy butter, and a big bowl of milk with a skin of cream on the top.

Carrie felt hollow with hunger. She said, 'I thought Mr Gotobed was dead. Mr Evans's sister's husband.'

'That's not him,' Albert said. 'Mister Johnny is a sort of distant cousin of *that* Mr Gotobed. He used to live in Norfolk but when his parents died he came here with Hepzibah. She's been his nurse since he was born.' He looked at Carrie as he set the candle down to give himself two free hands for the goose. 'Bit of a shock, I suppose, the first time.'

Holding the bag open so he could put the goose in, Carrie said, 'Is he mad?'

'No more than a lot of people. Just a bit simpler than some. Innocent, is what Hepzibah calls him.' Albert pushed the goose down and tied the string round the top of the bag. 'She's a witch,' he said calmly.

'A *witch*?'

He grinned at her. 'Oh, not what you're thinking of.

Not black cats and broomsticks! Just what country people call a wise woman. When I was ill she gave me some herbs made into a medicine and I got better quite quickly. The doctor was amazed – he had thought I was going to die. I never thought that lad would see the spring, was what he told Hepzibah.'

'So that's where you've been. In bed, ill!' Carrie said, and then blushed. This might sound, to Albert, as if she'd been looking for him. She said quickly, 'What's been wrong with you?'

'Pneumonia. Rheumatic fever,' Albert said. 'Just about every medical crime in the calendar. It's lucky I was sent here, to Hepzibah, or I'd be pushing up daisies. Though it wasn't luck, altogether. I told the billeting officer I liked books and he said there was a library here. And there is. A proper library, in a *house*!' He spoke as if this still amazed him. 'Shall I show you?'

They left the goose in the dairy and went back along the passage and through a swing door with baize on one side into a wide, dark hall where a grandfather clock ticked in one corner and a small oil lamp threw shadows. 'Here,' Albert said, opening another door and holding his candle high so that Carrie could see. Books – shelves and shelves of books, reaching up to the ceiling, most of them bound in pale calf with gold lettering on the spines. 'Marvellous, isn't it?' Albert said in a reverent voice as if he were speaking in church. 'And to think no one uses it! Only me!'

'Where's Mrs Gotobed?' Carrie asked.

'*Gone* to bed.' Albert laughed and his spectacles flashed. 'She's dying, I think.'

The idea of someone dying, here in this house, frightened Carrie. She looked up at the ceiling and shivered.

Albert said, 'She's been ill for ages. I read to her sometimes when she isn't too tired. Do you like reading?'

'Not much,' Carrie said. This wasn't quite true but all these books made her heart sink. So many words written; it would take a lifetime to read them.

'What do you do then?' Albert asked in a tone of surprise. 'When you're not at school, I mean.'

'I help in the shop sometimes. Mr Evans's shop. Nick's not allowed now, but I am. And I play on the mountains and I slide down the slag heap.'

Albert looked as if he thought these were rather childish occupations. But he said, politely and kindly, 'If you don't care for books much, perhaps you'd like to see the screaming skull. There's an interesting story about it. Untrue, I daresay, but interesting all the same.'

He advanced into the room and set the candle down on a desk. Carrie hung back. 'It sounds horrible.'

'Oh, it's only a skull,' Albert said. 'Come and see.'

There was a box on the desk and inside it, resting on velvet, a small, ivory skull. Pearly-smooth and grinning.

'Touch it,' Albert said, and Carrie touched the top lightly. It was warmer than she'd expected. She said, 'What's the story?'

'Ask Hepzibah,' Albert said. 'She tells it better than I

would. It's supposed to be the skull of an African boy who was brought here during the slave trade, but I don't believe it. It's not a boy's skull. You just look.'

He picked the skull out of its velvet bed and showed it to Carrie. The bottom jaw was missing and some of the teeth from the top, but the sockets were there. 'It had sixteen teeth in the top jaw,' Albert said, 'which means its wisdom teeth too. And you don't get your wisdom teeth until you're eighteen, at least. I looked it up in *Gray's Anatomy* and that's what it says. And you see those wiggly lines on the top? That's the sutures, where the bones are starting to join up. So it must have been a grown person's skull but it's too small and light for an adult male, so it must have been a woman. What I think is, there's an Iron Age settlement at the top of the Grove, and I think someone found this woman's skull there, and made up a story about it, the way people do.'

He put the skull back and looked at Carrie. 'That's *me* making up a story, of course. I don't *know*. But you can test the age of the bones. I'd like to take this skull to the British Museum one day and get them to test it. The British Museum can find anything out, it's the most marvellous place in the world. Have you been there?'

'Once,' Carrie said. She remembered going with her father one day, and being dreadfully bored. All those old things in glass cases. 'It's very interesting,' she said, to please Albert.

His eyes danced as if he guessed what she really had

thought. He put the skull back in its box and the lid on the top. He said, 'Would your brother like to see it?'

'No, he'd be scared,' Carrie said. 'That sort of thing scares him.'

Scared her a little too, though she wouldn't admit it to Albert. Not the skull, but the thought of the live person it had once been: a woman with eyes and hair who was dead now. Just pale, shiny bone in a box in a dark, musty library where the shelves of old books reached up into shadow. She said, 'Shouldn't we go back to the kitchen? I expect tea's ready by now.'

And it was. The cloth on the table was so stiffly starched that it stuck out at the corners. There was a huge plate of mince pies, golden brown and dusted with sugar, a tall jug of milk, a pink ham, and slices of bread thickly spread with the lovely, pale, sweaty butter Carrie had seen in the dairy. Nick was already at the table, tucking in, and Mister Johnny sat beside him, a white napkin round his neck. He chuckled excitedly as Carrie came in and she said, 'Hallo, Mister Johnny, can I sit next to you?'

Albert looked at her approvingly. He said, 'Hepzibah, I've been showing Carrie the skull. Tell her that old tale, will you? She'd like to hear it. Though it's a lot of old nonsense, of course!'

Hepzibah put a brown teapot down on the table and aimed a fake blow at his ear. 'I'll give you nonsense, my lad! Mister Albert Uppity-Know-All. You don't know so much yet, or you'd know that wise people don't mock what they don't understand!'

'Charsh, hcha,' Johnny Gotobed said.

'That's right, Mister Johnny.' Hepzibah bent over him, cutting up the ham on his plate. 'You've got more sense in your little finger than he's got in his clever young head.'

'I'm sorry, Hepzibah,' Albert said. 'Please tell Carrie.'

'Oh, it's a foolish tale, his young Lordship thinks.' Hepzibah sat down, smiling at Carrie and smoothing her copper hair back. She had a rather broad face, pale as cream, and dotted with freckles. Carrie thought she looked beautiful: so warm and friendly and kind.

She said, 'Please, Miss Green.'

'Hepzibah. That's my name.'

'Please, Hepzibah.'

'Well then. Perhaps I might, since you ask me so nicely. Fill up your plate now – go on, you can manage a bit more, growing girl like you. It's not home-cured ham, I'm sorry to say, though it would have been once. They had a good home farm, the Gotobeds. They made their money out of sugar and slaves and then moved here and made a fine place of the house. I heard about them long before I came to live here. When I was in service in Norfolk with Mister Johnny's parents, they used to tell me about their rich cousins in Wales and the screaming skull and the curse on the house. It's a queer old story, too . . .'

She sipped her tea thoughtfully, staring in front of her and frowning a little. Then she put her cup down and began to speak in a soft, sad, dreaming voice that seemed to weave a spell of silence in the room. 'He was brought here, the African boy, when he was ten or so. It was the fashion at that time for rich people to have a little black page, dressed up in silks and satins and riding on the step of their carriage. So they fetched this poor innocent away from his family, across the sea, to a strange land. And of course he cried, as any child might cry, taken from his mother. The Gotobeds weren't hard people, the young ladies gave him sweets and toys and made a real pet of him, but they couldn't comfort him, and in the end they said he could go back home one day. Perhaps they meant it, but he died of a fever his first winter here and it must have seemed to him that they'd broken a promise. So he put a curse on the house. He said, on his death-bed, that they could bury his body but when his flesh had rotted they must dig up his skull and keep it in the house or some dreadful disaster would come. The walls would crumble. And they believed him, people believed in curses then, and they did what he said. The skull has been kept in the library ever since – it only left the house once, when old Mr Gotobed's grandmother was a girl. She couldn't abide the thought of it, sitting there grinning, it gave her bad dreams she said, so she took it one morning and hid it in the stable loft. Nothing happened at all, she waited all day to see, and then went to bed, no doubt very pleased with herself. But in the middle of the night there was a great scream – like a screech owl – and a loud crashing sound. And when the family came running down in their night-clothes, all the crockery was smashed in the kitchen, all the glass in the dining-room, every mirror in the house cracked to pieces! Then of course the girl said what she'd done and they fetched the skull back and had no trouble after . . .'

'With sixteen teeth in its upper jaw,' Albert said. 'Count your teeth, Nick. You're the same age as that boy would have been, see if *you've* got sixteen!'

Nick blinked at him.

Carrie said, 'It's a lovely story, Albert Clever Sandwich, don't you dare spoil it!' Though she thought, secretly, that it was a comfort to know it might not be true. She said in a sentimental voice, 'A lovely *sad* story. Poor little African boy, all that way from home!'

Nick sighed, very deeply. Then he got down from his chair and went to stand by Hepzibah. He put his head on her shoulder and she turned and picked him up and sat him on her broad lap, her arms tight about him. She rocked him gently and he nestled close and put his thumb in his mouth. The room was quiet except for the hiss of the fire. Even Mister Johnny sat still, as if the story had lulled him, though perhaps it was only the soft sound of Hepzibah's voice.

Carrie looked at Nick on Hepzibah's lap and felt jealous. Of Nick, because she would like to be sitting there, she wasn't too big. And of Hepzibah, because she was comforting Nick in a way she knew she could never do.

She said, 'We ought to go, really. Auntie Lou knew we might stay to tea but it's getting late now and she'll start to worry.'

Then she thought of going back, through the dark trees, and her stomach seemed to sink down inside her. That noise she had heard, that deep, sighing breath!

Perhaps what she was feeling showed in her face because Albert said, 'I'll come with you if you like. As far as the railway.'

'Not with your chest, you won't,' Hepzibah said.

Albert grinned. 'I could hardly go without it, could I? Go on, Hepzibah, I'm strong as a horse now and I could do with some air.'

'Not night air,' Hepzibah said. 'Besides, I want you to come and read to Mrs Gotobed while I settle her, it puts her mind at rest for the night. Mister Johnny will see them safe through the Grove.' She smiled at Carrie, her eyes so bright, suddenly, that Carrie felt they saw straight into her mind. Though this was an odd feeling, it wasn't frightening somehow. Hepzibah said, 'You'll be all right with him. No harm of the kind you're afraid of, ever comes near the innocent.'

Carrie said, 'Mr Evans says no harm can ever come to those who trust in the Lord.'

'Perhaps that's another way of saying the same thing,' Hepzibah said. She gave Nick a last hug and tipped him off her lap. 'Come again, love. Both of you, whenever you like. Are you ready, Mister Johnny?'

He seemed to understand her. He was on his feet, holding out his hand to Nick who went to him and took it trustingly.

And so Mister Johnny took them up through the dark

yew trees, carrying the goose and holding Nick's hand. Carrie walked behind because there wasn't room for three on the path, but she wasn't afraid. Mister Johnny talked in his gobbly voice all the way and it seemed a friendly noise now, pushing the night back. Gobble-gobble, chuckle-chuckle – after a bit, to Carrie's surprise, Nick began to talk too, as if answering. He said things like, 'Yes, she was, wasn't she?' And, 'Oh yes, I'd *love* to do that.'

Carrie thought he was just being polite. But when they reached the railway line and Mister Johnny set the goose down and said, 'Gurlyi, gurlyi,' she knew what he was trying to say.

She said, 'Good-bye, Mister Johnny,' and smiled at him, and at first he tried to smile back, twitching the good side of his mouth. Then he covered his face with his small, fluttery hands and backed shyly away.

'Don't look straight at him like that,' Nick said. 'It upsets him, people looking. Good-bye, Mister Johnny.'

They took the goose between them and set off along the line that shone silver in the moonlight. When they put the heavy bag down for a rest and looked back, Mister Johnny had gone.

Carrie said, 'He was trying to say good-bye, wasn't he? You didn't understand anything else that he said, did you? Not really? I mean, I couldn't.'

'Only because you weren't listening,' Nick said, rather smugly.

'All right, then. What *did* he say? Come on, since you think you're so clever!'

'If you carry the goose. It's too heavy, it hurts my poor arm.'

'Baby!' But she picked the bag up and staggered along while Nick skipped beside her, jumping the sleepers.

He said, between jumps, 'He said a lot of things . . . He said we must come back again and he'd show us his cow . . . He said he'd show us his cow and then where the gulls nest, up on the mountain . . . He said he liked us and wanted us to come back, though he liked me the best . . . He said you were cross because I sat on Hepzibah's lap!'

'Liar,' Carrie said. 'You're making it up. What a mean, dirty trick!'

He looked at her slyly. 'Well, you were cross, weren't you?'

'Only because you're too old for that sort of thing. It made you look silly.'

'It didn't feel silly,' Nick said. 'It felt nice.'

Carrie looked at him and saw his mouth turning down at the corners.

Carrie said, 'Don't cry, I can't bear it. I wish we lived there, Albert Sandwich is *lucky*. But if we lived there, we wouldn't have it to look forward to, would we? I mean, we can look forward to going there, not every day of course, but once a week perhaps, and that'll be nice. Hepzibah did say we could go whenever we liked, didn't she?'

She put the goose down and looked at Nick. He said, 'Oh, Carrie, I don't *want* to look forward, I want

to be there all the *time*. I don't *want* to go back to the
Evanses', I really don't, I never did want to be there but
it's worse now, not better. I want to go *home* . . .'

Carrie knew what he meant. Sitting in that lovely,
bright, happy kitchen had made the Evanses' house
seem colder and bleaker than ever. But Nick was
working himself up into one of his states, and she had
to harden her heart.

She said, 'Then want must be your master, Nicholas
Peter Willow. Pull yourself together this minute, and
help me with this goose!'

CHAPTER 6

Mr Evans said, 'Did you see my sister? House in good order? Get a good tea?'

He fired these questions at them the moment they walked in the kitchen. His expression was eager and sly and it made Carrie cautious.

She said, '*She* was in bed. The house and the tea were all right.'

Nick looked surprised. 'Oh, Carrie, it was a lovely house. And a *lovely tea* Hepzibah gave us!' His eyes shone, remembering.

Mr Evans sucked his teeth and scowled. 'Better than you get here, I suppose? Oh, it's all right when you don't foot the bill, isn't it? That Miss Green! She'll not stint anyone, I daresay, but then it doesn't come out of her pocket! She doesn't have to sweat and slave for every penny!'

'Hepzibah's a good housekeeper, Samuel.' Pink patches appeared on Auntie Lou's neck as she looked at her brother. She moistened her lips and said pleadingly, 'She's been good to poor Dilys.'

Mr Evans snorted. 'And why shouldn't she be? She's on to a good thing and she knows it. A mistress too ill to keep her eye on the books! Feather her own nest if she chooses, and no one to know!'

Carrie felt her face go tight with anger but she said nothing. There are some things you know without being told and she knew Mr Evans was jealous of Hepzibah. Jealous of the way Nick's eyes had shone! It was always a mistake to let Mr Evans know you liked someone or had enjoyed anything. He didn't really care if she and Nick were happy or not but if he thought they had been happier at Druid's Bottom than they were at his house, he might stop them going again.

She said, 'I thought Hepzibah Green was *quite* nice. But the house is awfully old and dark and big, isn't it? and we *were* a bit scared of Mister Johnny!'

She thought her voice sounded put-on and silly – a silly, little girl's voice – but Mr Evans didn't seem to notice. Though Nick stared in bewilderment Mr Evans just said, 'So you saw the idiot, did you?'

Nick said in an outraged voice, 'Mister Johnny's not an idiot, he's not, he's *not*. I think you're just . . .'

He stopped and Carrie saw his mouth tremble while he searched for the right words to say how mean and horrible Mr Evans was. But perhaps he could think of no words bad enough because he began to cry instead, loud, gasping sobs, eyes wide and streaming.

Carrie said quickly, 'He's tired, he's just tired. It was an awful long walk, a bit too far for him, really. Come on, Nick, up to bed . . .'

She put her arm round his shoulders and hustled him out and upstairs before he recovered himself. But when he did, when they were safe in their bedroom with the door closed and the candle lit, it was her he was angry with.

'I think you're the meanest thing on this earth, Carrie Willow. A mean, ugly *cow*. Saying Hepzibah was *quite nice* in that voice!'

'I didn't mean . . .' Carrie began but he glared at her icily.

'I know what you meant. You're a traitor, that's what! A mean, horrible traitor and you're worse than *he* is. He's just nasty about everyone but you're nasty about people you *like* just to suck up to him! I hate him and I hate you and I won't *listen*!' And he flung himself down on his bed, his hands over his ears.

'It's not fair,' Carrie said. 'You're not fair.'

But there was no point in trying to explain, the mood he was in. She left him lying there and went down to say good night, treading on the paint at the side of the stairs to spare the carpet as Mr Evans had told her to do. She was half-way along the passage when his voice stopped her.

'Oh, the girl's got her head screwed on all right. Miss Green didn't take *her* in, did she, with her soft, smarmy ways? I tell you, Lou, it might be a good idea to get her to go there sometimes, keep her eyes open. I know what I *think* Miss Green's up to but I'd like to be sure.'

Auntie Lou said something that was too low for Carrie to hear and Mr Evans laughed. His voice was pitched higher than usual: more Welsh and excitable.

'Spying! What sort of word is that, girl? Am I the sort of man to set a child spying? Keep her eyes open, that's all I said, no harm in that, is it? It's Dilys I'm thinking of and you should give a thought to her, too. She's our own flesh and blood whatever she's done.'

Auntie Lou said, louder than before and in a voice that shook with boldness, 'That's the first time I've heard you say it, Samuel. For a good many long years.'

'Oh, I don't forgive her, that's one thing,' Mr Evans said. 'And it was one thing, see, when she had her pride and her strength. But that's gone from her now, isn't it? And it hurts me to think of her, helpless in that woman's power.'

Hepzibah's power? Did he mean Hepzibah was a witch, then? Albert had said that she was! Carrie stood shivering in the cold hall behind the half open door, wondering about Hepzibah and remembering her spell-binding voice telling that story about the old skull. And then felt, suddenly, that she was all the things Nick had said. A traitor, a mean, dirty traitor, standing here and listening and letting Mr Evans go on thinking that she hadn't liked Hepzibah. That she hadn't been taken in, was what he had said! Well, she would put that right now, this minute! March in and tell him, straight to his face! She drew a deep breath and ran into the kitchen and they turned in their chairs to look at her. Auntie Lou guiltily; Mr Evans with the angry red coming up in his face.

'What are you doing, girl? You went to bed, didn't you? Up and down, up and down, tramp, tramp, tramp on the carpet!'

'I walked on the paint,' Carrie said, but his face was almost purple by now and the veins stood out on his forehead as he half rose from his chair.

'Up and down, up and down, I won't have it, see? Back up with you now, double quick!' And as Carrie fled, his ranting voice followed her. 'Up and down, back and for, in and out, messing and humbugging about . . .'

Christmas came and went. Mr Evans was quite jolly on the Day itself, cracking jokes at dinner and giving presents, a knife for Nick and a Bible for Carrie. (The knife was a rather blunt penknife, not the sharp sheath knife Nick had hoped for, but it was better than nothing, and Carrie tried hard to be pleased with her Bible because Nick was grinning so slyly.) But the next day was doleful: Mr Evans in a bad mood because he had eaten too much and Auntie Lou tiptoeing about for fear of making things worse and so annoying him further. 'Creep, creep, creep,' he shouted at her, 'skitter, skitter, skitter. Are you a mouse, girl?'

Carrie and Nick would have escaped from the house if they could but it was bitterly cold and had begun to snow heavily. It snowed for three days without stopping, great cotton wool flakes, falling from a dark sky and swirling so thickly and blindingly that Mr Evans actually said the children need not use the privy in the yard in the daytime but could go up to the bathroom whenever they needed to.

On the fourth day they woke to sun and a white, dazzling world. 'Lovely day for a walk,' Mr Evans said heartily. 'Tell you what! Run along to Druid's Bottom and take Miss Green a tin of biscuits. A little present, see, to say thank you for the goose.'

Carrie looked at him sharply but he simply seemed to be in an unusually good temper. No reason, no reason at all for the odd, uncomfortable feeling inside her . . .

'Why should he want to send Hepzibah biscuits?' she said to Nick as they plodded through the deep snow at the side of the railway line, but he hadn't felt it was sinister.

'I expect they're stale,' he said cheerfully, 'and he's glad to be rid of them. Rid of us, too. She might give us lunch and that'll save him some money. Do you think she will, Carrie?'

'Don't you dare ask,' Carrie warned, but he stuck out his tongue and ran ahead, unafraid in the daylight, down the path through the Grove.

And of course it was the first thing Hepzibah said, turning pink and steamy from the stove and smiling as if it were the most natural thing in the world that Carrie and Nick should appear in her kitchen at precisely this minute. 'I was just dishing up. Nothing grand, mind, only roast pork and apple pie, but I expect you're hungry enough, this bitter cold day. Albert, set two more places.'

The lovely smell of roast pork made Carrie's mouth water but she said, very politely, 'Oh, I don't think we should. I mean, you weren't expecting us, were you?'

Albert said, 'How d'you know she wasn't? She's a witch, didn't I tell you? Besides, she likes to feed people. It's what she thinks people are *for*. Sometimes I think she doesn't look at their *faces*, just sees rows of empty stomachs to fill.'

'Take no notice of him,' Hepzibah said. 'Mr Too-Clever-By-Half. Take your coats off or you won't feel the benefit later.'

She was pleased with the biscuits. 'That's nice of Mr Evans. Lemon creams are Mister Johnny's favourites. Look, Mister Johnny, what the children have brought you!'

He stood in the corner of the kitchen, hanging his head and peeping through his fingers. But when Nick said, coaxingly, 'They're all for you, Mister Johnny,' he came forward slowly, smiling his lop-sided smile and gobbling softly with pleasure. Nick said, 'I promised we'd come again, didn't I?'

It was a lovely dinner. Carrie had two helpings of everything and Nick had three. They sat back as warm as toast and tight as drums and Hepzibah said, 'I've got to see to Mrs Gotobed now. Look after our guests, Mister Johnny.'

'Itchela-ka, itchela-ka.' He scrambled down from his chair and looked hopefully at Nick, and when he said, 'Do you mean you want us to come and help milk the cow?' Mister Johnny laughed and clapped his little hands together.

They went out in the cold afternoon. 'It must be below *zero*,' Albert said as they ran across the yard to the barn and the stables. The barn was full of roosting chickens, fluffed up against the cold, and there was an old cart horse and a cow in the stables; a fat, gentle-eyed Hereford. 'They used to have a prize herd,' Albert said. 'The Gotobed bulls were famous all over the world. But the family went downhill in the thirties – lost their money gambling and giving grand parties and travelling abroad, Hepzibah says – and in the end they had to sell most of their land, and the mine. Now there's only a couple of fields left, and one cow for the house. And not even enough money to repair the old generator, that's why we have oil lamps. We're too out of the way for mains electricity.'

'Scholly-ka, scholly-ka,' Mister Johnny said eagerly.

'Mister Johnny's cow,' Nick said. 'Is it your cow, Mister Johnny?'

'Scholly-ka.' Mister Johnny sat on a stool, his cheek pressed into the cow's smooth, swollen side as he milked her. She swished her tail and danced a little on her dainty back feet. He said, 'Letchely na, letchely na,' and she turned her beautiful head to look at him and lowed gently.

'She's due to calve next month,' Albert said. 'Have you ever seen a calf born?'

When the milking was done they collected the eggs, warm from scattered nests in the barn and the stable block, or snugly hidden in hedges. Mister Johnny knew where every nest was and chuckled proudly as he showed them. Albert said to Carrie, 'He even knows which time of the day each hen lays its egg, it's really *amazing*. They're like people to him, I suppose. Hepzibah says, give him a stray feather and he'll tell you which bird it comes from!'

Mister Johnny took the eggs and the pail of frothy milk and went into the house. The sun was dark red behind the trees now and their voices echoed in the valley as they slid on the frozen horse pond in the yard. Carrie was afraid at first that Albert would despise such a babyish pastime but he seemed to enjoy it as much as Nick did, shouting with laughter when he tripped over bumps in the ice and not wanting to stop, even when she said it was time they were going.

She left the two boys and went to say good-bye to Hepzibah. She wasn't in the kitchen, nor in the dairy where Mister Johnny was wiping the eggs and putting them into their trays. It was darker indoors than out and the oil lamp was already lit in the hall. Carrie peered into the dark library but there was no sign of Hepzibah. She waited a minute, then started to climb the smoothly polished, oak stairs, but stopped half-way up. Somewhere upstairs, someone was crying. Not as if they were in pain but very quietly and evenly, as if out of some dreadful and hopeless despair. Carrie thought it was the saddest sound she had ever heard. She stood still, feeling scared, and then, when Hepzibah appeared at the top of the stairs, ashamed too, as if she had no right to be listening.

Hepzibah said, 'Oh, it's you, Carrie.'

Her voice was pitched low and soft. Her spell-binding voice, Carrie thought, and looked up at her. She was holding a candle and her eyes shone in its light and her gleaming hair fell like silk on her shoulders. A beautiful witch, Carrie thought, and her heart began to thump so hard that she was sure Hepzibah must hear it. And if she did, she would look into Carrie's mind with her witch's eyes and know that she knew that it was Mrs Gotobed weeping upstairs, and that she was remembering what Mr Evans had said. *His own flesh and blood, his poor sister, helpless in that woman's Power!*

Hepzibah was coming down the stairs. She said, 'Carrie love, don't be frightened. It's only . . .'

But Carrie didn't want to hear. She said loudly, to cover the noise of her thumping heart, 'I'm not frightened, Hepzibah. I only came to say good-bye and thank you for a lovely day.'

It *had* been a lovely day and Nick sang all the way home because of it, one of his tuneless, made-up nonsense songs. 'We went to Druid's Bottom *and* we saw Mister Johnny, gobble-gobble-gobble, *and* we went milking the scholly-ka, *and* we had roast pork for dinner . . .'

While he sang, Carrie walked silently. The uncomfortable feeling she'd had earlier on had come back again and sat like a solid lead ball in her chest. She had done nothing wrong but she felt that she had. It wasn't always what you did but what you knew that was wicked! She had known why Mr Evans had sent Hepzibah biscuits; had known that he wanted her to spy, to keep her eyes open, and it seemed that without meaning to she had been doing just that! She felt mean and dirty – scared, too! Suppose, when they got back, he asked her what Miss Green was up to? Suppose he said, 'I know what's going on, did you find anything out?' Of course she didn't know anything and even if she did, she would rather die than say, but suppose he guessed she knew *something*? Suppose he tortured her to make her tell!

But when they got back, he barely spoke to them. He was in one of his sour silent moods and when Nick said, 'Hepzibah said thank you very much for the biscuits,' he only grunted in answer. Carrie thought, perhaps he's waiting till Nick's gone to bed! Perhaps he'll come into the room when Nick's fast asleep and bend over me and say, 'Well, girl, how's my sister?'

She lay awake until he came up but he passed their door without stopping and she heard *his* door close and the jangle of springs through the wall as he sat on the bed to take his boots off. She thought, perhaps he's waiting till the next time we go, perhaps he's biding his time . . .

He didn't seem to be. He asked no questions about

Druid's Bottom, about what they had done, or what they had seen. Not that time, nor the next time they went; nor the next, nor the next . . .

Until, in the end, Carrie began to think she must have made it all up, that she had just dreamed all those things he had said. And as the weeks went by it grew into that. A bad dream, almost forgotten . . .

CHAPTER 7

January snowed itself out. Auntie Lou's cold 'hung on', as she put it, and she went to stay with a friend in the bigger town down the valley. She stayed for four days and Carrie did the cooking at home. Mr Evans only complained once, about burnt potatoes, and when Auntie Lou came back, he said, 'That girl's a better cook than you'll ever be.' Carrie thought this was rude but Auntie Lou didn't seem to mind. She was much better, hardly coughing at all, and she sang while she worked in the kitchen.

February came, and the calf was born at Druid's

Bottom. It was born on a Sunday afternoon and Carrie and Albert and Nick saw it happen. The cow lowing and lowing and Mister Johnny talking to her in his soft, bubbly voice, and pulling on the little hooves when they slowly appeared. And the astonishingly big calf coming out with a slippery rush and then, a few minutes later, standing up in the straw on its thin, wobbly legs, its thickly lashed eyes mild and brown like its mother's.

'I've never seen anything so exciting in my whole life,' Nick said afterwards. 'It's my *best thing*!'

'I shouldn't tell Mr Evans you saw the calf born,' Carrie said.

'Why not?'

'Just because.'

'Well, I did see it, didn't I? *And* my chilblains are better, too,' Nick said, happily counting his blessings. 'That's the magic ointment Hepzibah gave me.'

'Not magic, just herbs,' Carrie said, though she wasn't too sure about this. 'And I shouldn't tell Auntie Lou it was Hepzibah. She thinks it's those gloves that she gave you, keeping you warm.'

'I know she does.' Nick smiled, smugly and sweetly. 'That's what I told her, you silly dope. D'you think I'm an idiot?'

February turned into March and Albert came back to school. Although he was only eighteen months older than Carrie he was in the top class and sometimes he was taught on his own by Mr Morgan, the Minister, because he was cleverer than even the most senior boys. But he wasn't stuck up about this, nor did he ignore Carrie and Nick when other people were there. He didn't seem to care that Nick was so much younger than he was. He would turn up in the Primary School playground and call, 'Hi there, Nick!' as if Nick was a boy the same age. 'I don't see what difference it makes, people's ages,' he said when Carrie told him the girls in her class thought this odd. 'People are either your friends or they aren't. Nick's my friend, and Hepzibah. And Mrs Gotobed too, and she's *ancient*.'

April – and Carrie met Mrs Gotobed. On the first day of the Easter holidays, Mister Johnny took Nick up the mountain to where the gulls nested, on an island in a small lake. They often went on excursions, always talking away nineteen to the dozen. Sometimes Nick understood what Mister Johnny said and sometimes he only pretended he did, to annoy Carrie, but they were always happy together. Happier alone, Carrie knew, than when she was with them, and although she didn't really mind this, it made her feel lonely this particular day. Albert was reading in the library because Mr Morgan was coming to give him an extra Greek lesson and Hepzibah was busy, bustling in and out of the kitchen with no time for Carrie. She sat by the fire and pretended she was quite happy alone, just sitting quietly and thinking, but Hepzibah knew better. She looked up from the tray she was laying – silver teapot and best china and thin bread and butter – and said, 'What's up with you, Miss Down-In-The-Mouth? Nothing to do, is that it? Well, you can go and keep Mrs Gotobed company. I'll put another cup on the tray and you can have tea with her.' She smiled at Carrie's horrified face. 'It's all right, she won't bite you.'

Mrs Gotobed was downstairs in a room Carrie had not been into before; a light, pretty drawing-room, all gilt chairs and mirrors. A wing-chair was drawn up to a crackling wood fire and Mrs Gotobed sat in it. At first Carrie hardly dared look at her but when she did she saw nothing alarming or sinister, just an old lady with silvery hair piled up high and a pale, invalid's face. She held out a thin hand covered with huge, glittering rings that were loose on her fingers and said, 'Come and sit here, pretty child. On this stool. Let me look at your eyes. Albert says they're like emeralds.'

'Oh,' Carrie said. She blushed and sat, very straight-backed, on the stool.

'Handsome is as handsome does,' Hepzibah said. She put the tray on a low table and left them together.

Mrs Gotobed smiled and her face crinkled up like pale paper. 'Hepzibah thinks looks don't matter much but they do, you know. Do you like my dress?'

She was wearing what seemed to be a red silk ball gown, embroidered with silver flowers on the bodice and very long and full in the skirt. 'It's lovely,' Carrie said, though she thought it a strange dress for someone to wear in the daytime.

Mrs Gotobed's hands, stroking her silken skirt, made a faint, rasping sound. 'My husband gave it to me just after we married,' she said. 'We bought it in Paris and I had to stand for hours while they fitted me. My waist was so small, they said they had never seen anyone with such a small waist. Mr Gotobed could hold it in his two hands. He loved buying me clothes, he bought me twenty-nine ball gowns, one for each year of our marriage and I have them all still, hanging up in my closet. I put on a different one each time I get up. I want to wear each one of them once more before I die.'

All the time she was talking her thin hands stroked the silk of her dress. *She's mad,* Carrie thought, *raving mad . . .*

'Pour the tea, child,' Mrs Gotobed said. 'And I'll tell you about my dresses. I've got a green chiffon with pearls sewn round the neck and a blue brocade and a grey silk with pink ostrich feathers. That was my husband's favourite so I'm keeping that one till the last. I looked like a Queen in it, he always said . . . Just a little milk in my tea, and two slices of bread, folded over.'

Her eyes were pale grey and bulging a little. Like Mr Evans's eyes, Carrie thought, but apart from her eyes she didn't look in the least like a shopkeeper's sister. Sitting in that grand dress, in this beautiful room . . .

'Would you like jam?' Carrie asked. 'It's Hepzibah's blackberry.'

'No, child. No jam.' Mrs Gotobed looked at Carrie with Mr Evans's pale eyes and said, 'So you're my brother's evacuee, God help you!'

Carrie stiffened. 'I like Mr Evans,' she found herself saying.

'Then you're the only one does. Cold, hard, mean man, my brother. How d'you get on with my baby sister, Louisa?'

'Oh, Auntie Lou's *nice*,' Carrie said. She looked at Mrs Gotobed's claw-like, ringed fingers holding her delicate cup, and thought of Auntie Lou's little red hands that were always in water, washing dishes or scrubbing floors or peeling potatoes.

'Nice, but a fool,' Mrs Gotobed said. 'No spunk, or she'd have left *him* long ago. She'll lie down and let him walk over her till the end of her days. Does he walk over you?'

Carrie shook her head firmly.

'Not afraid of him? Well, if you're not, then you can tell him something from me.' She sipped her tea and looked so long and thoughtfully into the fire that Carrie began to think she had forgotten her. She had finished all the bread and butter and scraped the dish of blackberry jam before Mrs Gotobed turned from the fire and spoke again, very slowly and clearly. 'When I die,' she said, 'you can tell him from me that I hadn't forgotten him. That I hadn't forgotten he was my own flesh and blood, but that sometimes you owe more to strangers. That I've done what I've done because it seemed to me right, not because I wanted to spite him.' She put her cup down and laughed softly and her eyes shone like pale stones under water. 'Only wait till I'm safely dead first! Or he'll be round here, stamping and yelling and I haven't the strength for it.' She waited a minute, then said, 'Do you understand what I've told you?'

Carrie nodded but the nod was a lie. She didn't understand but she felt too embarrassed to say so. Mrs Gotobed was embarrassing, talking in that dreadful, calm way about dying, as if she were saying, 'When I go on holiday.'

Carrie couldn't even look at her. She stared at her hands, her ears burning. But Mrs Gotobed said nothing more and when Carrie did look, she was lying back in her chair with her head fallen sideways. She was lying so still Carrie thought she was dead, but when she got up to run and call Hepzibah she saw that her chest was still moving and knew she was only asleep. She ran all the same, out of the room, across the hall, into the kitchen. She said, '*Hepzibah!*' and Hepzibah came to her. Held her close for a minute, then lifted her chin and looked into her face. 'It's all right,' Carrie stammered, 'she's just gone to sleep,' and Hepzibah nodded and touched her chin lightly and lovingly and said, 'I'd best go to her then, you stay here with Albert.'

When she had gone, Albert said, from the fire, 'Did she frighten you?'

'No,' Carrie said. But she had been frightened and it made her angry with Albert. 'I thought she was dead and that's your fault! You told me she was dying when we first came. Months ago!'

'She is dying,' Albert said. 'D'you mean I shouldn't have told you?'

Carrie wasn't sure what she did mean. She said, 'She shouldn't talk about it.'

Albert looked surprised. 'I don't see why not. It's fairly important to her.'

'It's horrible,' Carrie said. '*She's* horrible. Spooky! Dressing up in all those grand clothes when she's dying!'

'It cheers her up to put them on,' Albert said. 'It was her life, you see, parties and pretty clothes, and putting them on makes her remember how happy she used to be. It was my idea, as a matter of fact. When I came here, she was so miserable. Crying all the time! One evening she told Hepzibah to show me her dresses and cried because she'd never wear them again. I said, why not, and she said because there was no point, no one to see, and I said *I'd* like to see them. So she puts a dress on, when she feels well enough, and I go and look and she talks to me about the times she wore it before. It's quite interesting really.'

He spoke as if this were a perfectly natural thing to do. Carrie thought of it, of the sick old woman dressing up in her jewels and her beautiful clothes, and of this skinny, solemn, bespectacled boy watching her, and it didn't seem natural at all. She said, 'You are funny, Albert. Funny peculiar, I mean. Not ordinary.'

'I would hate to be ordinary,' Albert said. 'Wouldn't you?'

'I don't know,' Carrie said. Albert seemed so grown up suddenly, it made her feel silly and young. She wanted to tell him the rest of it; tell him what Mrs

Gotobed had told her to tell Mr Evans and ask Albert what he thought she had meant, but she couldn't think how to put it without making herself sound fearfully stupid. And then, a few minutes later, Nick came bursting in with Mister Johnny behind him and there was no time to say anything.

Nick was excited. 'Oh, it was marvellous, Carrie! The lake, and the white gulls, and the brown island. I couldn't see anything at first and Mister Johnny said, sit still and wait, and I *sat* still, and then the island sort of *moved*. And the brown part wasn't the *earth*, but thousands and thousands of baby gulls, packed so tight you couldn't see the grass under them! Oh, Carrie, it's my *best thing*. The best thing in my whole life!'

'Like the calf being born. And your tenth birthday gloves. You're always having *best things*,' Carrie said, rather sourly.

'I can't help it, can I?' Nick looked puzzled and hurt. Then smiled suddenly. 'It'll be your turn next, won't it? It's your birthday next month!'

Carrie's birthday was at the beginning of May. Mr Evans and Auntie Lou gave her handkerchiefs and her mother sent her a green dress that was too tight in the chest and too short. Auntie Lou said she could sew a piece of material on the bottom to lengthen the skirt but there was nothing she could do about the top and Carrie cried a little, privately, not because the dress was no use but because her mother should have guessed how much she had grown. She felt miserable about this all the morning, but better in the afternoon when they went to Druid's Bottom after school. Hepzibah had cooked a cake with white icing and twelve candles and Mister Johnny made her a crown of wild flowers to put on her head.

'Now you're the Queen of the May,' Hepzibah said.

She wore the crown while they sat in the sunshine, eating the cake, but by the time they went home it was already wilting a little.

Albert walked them up through the Grove. 'You should soak it in the Sacred Spring,' he said. 'Then maybe it'll last for ever.'

He didn't seem to be teasing. Carrie said, 'You don't believe that?'

Albert shrugged his shoulders. 'Hepzibah half does. She fills bottles from the spring sometimes, to make medicines. She says it's because the water is pure from the mountain but she doesn't really believe it's just that. And perhaps it isn't. She put some spring water on my wart one evening and it was gone when I woke the next day.'

'Beans will do that,' Carrie said. 'Or fasting spit. Nick had a wart and he spat on it first thing every morning and by the end of the week it was gone.'

'That's magic,' Albert said. 'The spring is Religion. That's different.'

'D'you mean the *old religion*?' Carrie laughed, to show she thought this was nonsense. 'That's what Auntie Lou calls it, but then she's a bit silly.'

'Oh, I don't know,' Albert said. 'No one knows,

really. Only that this was a Sacred Place once. Not just the Grove, the whole mountain. They found an old temple, just a few stones and some old bones – that's where I think the skull came from, d'you remember I told you? But they've found similar temples in other parts of the world, the same sort of arrangement of stones, so they think this religion must have been everywhere once.'

Carrie felt cold, though it was a warm day and above their heads, above the dark yews, the sun was still shining. She whispered – she didn't mean to whisper but she couldn't help it – 'The first time we came, when we were so scared, it wasn't just Mister Johnny. I thought I heard something before I heard him. A sort of big sigh. As if something were breathing. Don't laugh!'

'I'm not,' Albert said. 'It's as silly to laugh as it is to be scared. There's nothing to be scared of, any more than in an old church. I think it's just that places where people have believed things have an odd feel to them . . .' He was quiet for a little, then whispered, as Carrie had done, 'Unless there *is* something else. Some secret Power, sleeping . . .'

'You're scared yourself!' Carrie said, and he did laugh at her then. It was easy to laugh because they were at the top of the path now, coming out of the Grove into sunlight.

A train was coming out of the tunnel. It rattled past them, blowing their clothes and their hair. Nick was some way along the line, at the bend where the track curved round the mountain and Carrie saw him put his hands over his ears as the train blew its whistle. 'Poor Nick,' she said, 'he does hate it.'

Albert said, 'Carrie . . .' and she turned and saw his face close to hers. He kissed her, bumping her nose with his glasses, and said, 'Happy Birthday.'

Carrie couldn't think what to say. She said, 'Thank you,' very politely.

'Girls don't say thank you when they get kissed.' Though Albert spoke in a calm, schoolmastery tone, his colour had risen. He turned away, to hide this, perhaps; waved once, without looking, and ran down the path. As soon as he was out of sight he began to sing, very loudly.

Carrie sang too, as she skipped down the railway track; sang under her breath and laughed to herself. When she caught up with Nick, he said, 'What are you laughing for?'

'I can laugh, can't I?' Carrie said. 'There's no law against it? Have you heard of a law against laughing, Mr Clever-Dick-Nick?'

But there was one, it seemed. Not a real law of course, but a rule Carrie had made up for herself and had stuck to, until she forgot it today. Forgot that it was a mistake to let Mr Evans see she was happy . . .

She went hop, skip, and jump down the hilly street and through the shop door. Laughter was bubbling up inside her and when Mr Evans looked up and said, 'Oh, it's you then,' it seemed to spill over.

She said, 'Who did you think it was, the cat's mother?' and this silly joke made her laugh till her eyes ran with water.

He stared at her, and when he spoke his voice was dangerously quiet. 'Whatever's got into you, girl?'

Even then she wasn't warned. She was silly with happiness. She said, 'Nothing, Mr Evans, just nice things, that's all,' and ran through the shop into the kitchen.

He followed her. She stood at the sink, running the tap to get a glass of cold water and he stood behind her. She filled the glass and drank. He said, 'Taken your time, haven't you? Other people in the world beside yourself, you know. Waiting for their tea.'

The water ran down inside Carrie like a lovely cold pipe, making her gasp. When she could speak, she said, 'I told Auntie Lou we were going to see Hepzibah straight after school. We're not late.'

She saw Auntie Lou had laid tea: a clean cloth, a plate of sandwiches, covered over, and a small cake with candles.

Mr Evans sucked his teeth and his pale eyes bulged coldly. 'Oh no, not at all. Come and go as it suits you. Liberty Hall, that's what you've made of my home! Your birthday tea ready but you were having a better time somewhere else! Oh, don't trouble to answer. It's written all over you!'

'I said we'd be back by half past six and we are,' Carrie said.

'Oh, *ordering* your meals now, is it? Servants at your

beck and call, that's our place! And no gratitude – your Auntie can slave for you, work her fingers to the bone, but it's Miss Green gets the thank yous! And what for, may I ask? Easy enough to keep open house when someone else pays, isn't it? Miss Green can ask in what riff-raff she chooses! Everyone welcome and no bills presented!'

Carrie said, 'It's only me and Nick ever go there.'

'Have you been *invited*, though? My sister's house, isn't it? She ever invite you? That doesn't worry you, I suppose, since you've never seen her. And that suits *Miss Green*, doesn't it? To keep the poor soul shut away out of sight, out of mind!'

'She's not shut away, she's just ill,' Nick shouted. He had been listening from the doorway; now he marched into the room and glared at Mr Evans, his eyes hot with anger. He said, 'And Carrie has seen her, so there!'

Mr Evans looked at Carrie and his look made her tremble. She said faintly, 'Only just once.'

'And why didn't you tell me?'

'I didn't think . . .'

'Didn't think! Didn't think *what*! I'm not supposed to be interested, is it? My own flesh and blood and I'm not interested to hear of her?'

'There wasn't anything to say.'

'She said nothing, did she? Sat dumb? No message for me, for her brother?'

Carrie felt as if she were suffocating. Mr Evans's face seemed to hang over her, pale and sweaty, like cheese. He said, 'Come on, don't lie to me, girl!'

Carrie shook her head. She couldn't speak. This was like a bad dream coming true. Feeling so frightened without quite knowing why, and Mr Evans's pale eyes boring into her, and no escape anywhere . . .

It was Auntie Lou saved her. Nick said in a shrill voice, 'That's a new blouse, Auntie Lou,' and Mr Evans turned from Carrie to look at his sister.

She was standing in the doorway and smiling uncertainly. The new blouse was pink and frilly, quite unlike anything the children had seen her wear before, and she had combed her hair and put lipstick on. She looked quite different. She looked almost pretty.

Mr Evans said in an awful voice, 'A frivolous woman is an abomination in the sight of the Lord.'

Auntie Lou's smile vanished but she said, bravely, 'Do you like my blouse, Nick? It's the one my friend gave me when I went to stay with her. She gave me the lipstick, too.'

'LIPSTICK!' Mr Evans said.

Auntie Lou gave a tiny laugh. 'Most girls wear lipstick, Samuel. I didn't want to be different when we went to the dance.'

'DANCE!'

'At the Camp.' Auntie Lou's voice was a whisper, a thin thread of sound. 'The American Base, down the valley.'

'AMERICAN SOLDIERS!' Mr Evans bellowed. Then he turned on the children. 'Out of here, both of you. I have a few things to say to my sister.'

They fled from the kitchen, down the yard to the

sunny patch at the side of the privy. Out of sight of the house though not out of earshot. Not that they needed to hear what Mr Evans had to say because they had heard it before. Girls who wore lipstick and silly clothes and went out with American soldiers were good as damned in his opinion. And Auntie Lou knew it.

Carrie said, 'She must be stark mad to come in and let him see her like that. She knows what he's like.'

'She only did it to take him off you,' Nick said. 'To stop him bullying you on your birthday.'

'*Oh*,' Carrie said. And then, 'How long will he go on, d'you think?'

'Just till she cries. Then he'll make her wash her face and we can have tea. You hungry, Carrie?'

'No.'

'I'm not either. I couldn't swallow.' He sat hunched up, listening to the steady roar from the kitchen. He said, 'Getting used to things doesn't make them any better, does it? He's a horrible, disgusting, yakky hog-swine. What was he on at you about? What did he want you to tell him?'

'I don't know.'

'You do, then.' Nick looked at her. 'I could tell by your face that you did! So could he, I expect!'

Carrie groaned. 'Aaaaaaaaoooooooooooow . . .' shutting her eyes and stretching her arms out sideways and stiff till her shoulder blades hurt. Then she collapsed limply, put her head on her knees, and said, 'I think he wants me to tell him something nasty about Hepzibah.

Like she's cruel to his sister. But that's only part of it.'
She thought of the message Mrs Gotobed had asked
her to take to her brother, and then, because it
frightened her to think about this, said loudly and
passionately, 'I won't spy for him, I won't, I *won't*. I
won't tell him *anything*.'

'Keep your hair on, girl,' Nick said in a mild,
surprised voice. 'You don't have to, do you? I mean, he
can't *make* you.'

'I don't know,' Carrie said. 'I don't know.'

CHAPTER 8

Carrie said to Hepzibah, 'Mr Evans hates the Americans. Auntie Lou was going to see her friend yesterday but he wouldn't let her because once when she went, she and this friend went to a dance with some American soldiers. I don't see why he feels like that, do you? I mean it's a good thing the Americans have come, isn't it? To help us fight Hitler?'

Hepzibah was ironing. She and Carrie were alone in the kitchen. As there was no electricity at Druid's Bottom, Hepzibah used two flat irons, heating them in turn on the fire. When one cooled she picked up the other and spat to test it. She did this now and the spit sizzled on the iron. She said, 'The Americans are better off than we are, that's why. Mr Evans can't abide that, people being well off and throwing their money about.'

'Mr Evans is *mean*,' Carrie said. Poor Auntie Lou, she had cried! The tears had run down her face as she stood at the sink, washing up after tea. Thinking about it made Carrie feel chokey inside, and helpless, and angry. She said, 'Mrs Gotobed says he's a mean, cold, hard man.'

'He's had a cold, hard life and it's made him cold and hard,' Hepzibah said. She was ironing one of Mister Johnny's shirts and a warm, starchy smell filled the kitchen. 'He saw his dad die down the pit and he couldn't save him. He came up and swore he'd never go down again, it was no life for an animal! And he stuck to that. He got a job at the grocer's shop, dogsbody work, sweeping up and delivering, but he saved every penny he could till he had enough to put down, with a loan from the Bank, to buy the place up. His wife was no help to him, she was a poor, sickly creature, and he had his young sister to care for beside his own boy. Mrs Gotobed would have taken the girl, but he wouldn't allow it. The Gotobeds led a bad life to his strict way of thinking, gambling and travelling and pleasuring themselves, and he said Louisa should be brought up in the fear of the Lord.'

'Poor Auntie Lou,' Carrie said.

'Who's to say? I don't know she'd have been better off here. Rich people's charity can be a cold business.'

Hepzibah sounded as if she knew about this. She folded the shirt she was ironing and pressed the collar flat. Then smiled at Carrie. 'Whatever the rights and wrongs of *that* matter, Mr Evans has had a hard, lonely fight and it's made him bitter against those who haven't. It's what he's got against Mrs Gotobed, when you come down to it. Her life's been too easy.'

Carrie said, 'Auntie Lou said he was angry with her because she married the mine-owner's son. She says they were bad owners and it was their fault his dad died.'

'That was part, perhaps,' Hepzibah said. 'But it was mostly the other thing, that he'd had to sweat all his life and she'd never done a hand's turn. She rose up in the world without lifting a finger when she married into the gentry and I daresay she let him feel the difference between them. When I first came here with Mister Johnny – *he* was only a little lad then and I wasn't much older – the Gotobeds still had their money and they kept house in style. Butler and cook and parlour maids and a bailiff for the farm! Most of the groceries came down from a grand shop in London but she'd order perishable goods from her brother and then send a servant to complain of the quality. And he'd send messages back through his delivery boy! Never a word passed directly between them! They were two of a kind, people said. Peacock proud and stubborn with it, neither giving an inch. That's the trouble now, really. She's fond of him still, in her way, but they quarrelled all those years ago and it's too late to mend it. He'll never forgive her for the life she has spent and she won't let him see what she's come to at the end of it! Poor as a church mouse by *her* standards, and weak as a kitten!'

It seemed a sad story to Carrie. She told Nick and said, 'Don't let's ever quarrel like that.'

'Why should we?'

'I don't know. Just let's *not*.'

'I won't if you won't.

'Promise?'

'Oh, all right.' Nick looked bored but he licked his forefinger and drew it across his throat.

Carrie did the same. Then sighed. 'I'm sorry for Mr Evans, really.'

'You must be out of your mind,' Nick said. 'Stark raving bally-bonkers.'

Two days later they were alone in the house when the shop bell jangled. Carrie went to open it and an American soldier stood there. He was very tall and very polite, taking his cap off before he said, in a soft, drawly voice, 'Major Harper, Ma'am. Major Cass Harper. Is Miss Louisa Evans at home?'

Mr Evans was at a Council meeting and Auntie Lou was at the Chapel, cleaning up for Sunday. Carrie said, 'There's just me and Nick at the moment.'

Major Harper smiled and his eyes crinkled up. He was quite old, Carrie decided, looking at the creases in his pink, cushiony cheeks and the way his hair was going thin at the sides. He said, 'Then may I come in and wait till Miss Louisa comes home?'

No one ever came to the Evanses' house to visit. Auntie Lou had friends in the town who asked her to tea sometimes but she never dared ask them back. 'Once you let people get a foot in the door there's no end to it,' was what Mr Evans said. 'Traipsing in and out, up and down, back and for, all day and all night . . .'

Just to think of what he would say if he came home from a Council meeting and found an American soldier sitting in his parlour made Carrie's stomach shrivel. She said, 'Oh no, you can't do that, I'm afraid. Mr Evans might come back first, you see.'

Major Harper looked politely surprised. 'Miss Louisa's brother? Why, I'd be glad to get acquainted with him.'

'He might not be glad, though,' Carrie said miserably. 'He doesn't — he doesn't like American soldiers. It's nothing personal. I mean, I'm sure you're awfully nice, it's not that . . .'

She was afraid Major Harper would be angry but he only smiled, blue eyes twinkling. 'I'm a very respectable American soldier,' he said.

He *was* nice, Carrie thought. So nice that it would be quite awful if Mr Evans were to turn up and start shouting at him. It would upset Major Harper and it would upset Auntie Lou, and all to no purpose because Mr Evans would never let her see him again.

She said, 'There's no point in your staying, really

there isn't. It wouldn't be any good at all. Even if you did see her, Mr Evans wouldn't let you go out with her, to a dance, or the pictures, or *anything*. Mr Evans says dance halls and cinemas are haunts of the Devil and a frivolous woman is an abomination in the eyes of the Lord.'

Major Harper had stopped smiling. His plump, rosy face was very solemn indeed and so was his voice. 'Miss Louisa is a lovely, gracious lady and I wouldn't wish to be a trouble to her.'

'You would be, I'm afraid,' Carrie said. 'He'd make her cry. He's always making her cry.'

'I see,' Major Cass Harper said. 'I'm obliged to you for explaining the situation. Perhaps you'll say . . .' He paused, as if wondering what Carrie could tell Auntie Lou. 'Tell her I called,' he said. 'Just that. And that I'm real sorry I missed her.'

Carrie watched him go up the steep main street. An Army car was parked outside the Dog and Duck and he disappeared into the pub without looking back. Carrie closed the shop door and Nick said, 'Why, you rotten, *mean* . . .' He was standing just behind her and his face was scarlet. 'You rotten, mean *pig*. That's her *friend* come to see her and you sent him away!'

'I couldn't ask him in, could I? Suppose Mr Evans came back?'

'Mr Evans, Mr Evans, all you think about's Mr Evans! What about poor Auntie Lou?'

'There'd be a row and she'd cry,' Carrie said. 'I can't bear it when she cries.'

'*You* can't bear it? What's that got to do with her? Maybe she'd rather see her friend first, even if she had to cry after,' Nick said. 'I'm going to tell her.'

And he pushed past her and opened the door and started running down the street towards the War Memorial Square and Ebenezer Chapel. Carrie hesitated, but only a second, and then she ran after him. She called, 'Wait for me, Nick,' and he looked back and grinned at her.

It was cold in the Chapel, like going into a tunnel. Auntie Lou was on her knees scrubbing the floor of the aisle. She sat back on her heels, pushing her hair back with her wrist as they raced up to her.

'Your friend's come,' Carrie said. 'Major Cass Harper.'

'*Oh*,' Auntie Lou said. She just sat and stared at them.

'He's in the Dog and Duck. Hurry up, or he'll go.'

Auntie Lou got to her feet and put her hands up to her hair again. Her hands were shaking like red autumn leaves but her bright eyes were shining.

'Don't fuss with your hair, it's all right,' Nick said. 'Just take your apron off, you'll look all right then.'

She unfastened her apron and folded it and looked down at herself. 'Oh,' she moaned, 'my old skirt!'

'He won't mind that, he's too nice,' Carrie said.

Auntie Lou wrung her red hands together. 'I can't – *I can't* go into the Dog and Duck. Mr Evans . . .'

'Won't know if you don't tell him,' Carrie said. 'No one else will, that's for sure.'

She hoped this was true. Nothing that went on in the town was a secret for long. And there were plenty of people who would be pleased to tell Councillor Evans that his sister had been seen in the Dog and Duck with an American soldier. Not to hurt Auntie Lou, everyone liked Auntie Lou, but to get their own back on *him* . . .

'The floor!' Auntie Lou said. 'I haven't finished the floor!'

'We'll do it,' Nick said. And added, in a fair imitation of Mr Evans's voice, 'Get on if you're going! Double-quick now!'

They scrubbed the tiles and put the bucket and cloths away in the little room at the back of the Chapel where the flower pots were kept and the Minister's clothes. Then they walked slowly back to the shop. There was no sign of the Army car outside the Dog and Duck but Auntie Lou wasn't at home. Only Mr Evans, doing his accounts in his office. He said, 'Where's your Auntie?'

'It's a lovely evening,' Carrie said. 'She went for a walk up the mountain. I said I'd get supper.'

She laid the table in the kitchen, putting out the bread and a big bowl of dripping, and then made the cocoa. The light was fading outside. Nick whispered, 'D'you think she'll come *back*?'

Carrie took Mr Evans's cocoa into the office. He sat back, rubbing his eyes. They looked red and sore and his mouth seemed to droop at the corners. 'Figures,

figures, figures,' he said. 'No end to it. No rest for the righteous!'

'Must you work so hard?' Carrie said, thinking of the things Hepzibah had told her, how he'd worked all his life and had no help from anyone, and he looked at her with surprise.

'Sympathy, is it? That's something I don't often get!' Then he smiled – not one of his tigerish grins but a perfectly ordinary, rather tired smile – and said, 'No help for it, is there, with this old war on? Can't even get a boy to deliver! But the only things worth having are the things you've worked hard for, and I'll last out, I daresay, so don't you worry, girl! Go and see to young Nicodemus and have your own supper!'

Carrie lingered, partly because she felt so sorry suddenly, and partly because she felt guilty. She had told him a lie about Auntie Lou going for a walk up the mountain and Auntie Lou didn't know what she'd said. Suppose she came back now and told him she'd been somewhere else? It would be dreadful to be caught out in a lie; dreadful at any time, but worse now, when he was being so friendly. She said, 'Can I help you add up? I'm quite good at maths, it's my best subject at school.' That was another lie, and her cheeks reddened with the shame of it, but he didn't notice because the shop bell had tinkled.

The door opened and closed. Quick, light steps though the shop, and Auntie stood in the office. She was smiling and her whole face shone as if candles had been lit inside her. Like a turnip head at Hallow E'en,

Carrie thought. She watched Mr Evans turn in his chair and look up at his sister and felt her chest tighten. What was it the air-raid wardens shouted when they saw a house with a chink of light showing? *Put that light out!* 'Oh, put it out, Auntie Lou,' Carrie shouted, inside her, and said, aloud, 'Was it nice, up the mountain?'

Auntie Lou looked at her vaguely as if Carrie spoke some strange, foreign language. Or as if she herself had just returned from another world altogether. 'Don't be stupid now, Auntie Lou,' Carrie prayed, but knew it was hopeless. Mr Evans was bound to find out and there would be a terrible row. He would know she had lied to him, and be hurt, and never trust her again . . .

She stood with her head bowed, waiting for the story to break over it. But all he said was, 'Oh, it's all right for some, isn't it? Messing and humbugging about all hours of the night! Clear off and get your supper, the pair of you. Some of us have to work for our living!'

CHAPTER 9

Carrie didn't see Major Cass Harper again, but Nick did. Sliding the slag heap one day after school, he looked across the mountain and saw Auntie Lou and a soldier sitting on the grass by the side of a stream. An American Army car was parked on the road just below them. 'They didn't see me,' he told Carrie.

'If I were you, I'd forget you saw *them*,' she said. 'Suppose Mr Evans starts asking us questions? Where she is, what's she up to, that sort of thing? Best to pretend we don't know.'

Though they couldn't help knowing. Auntie Lou

was so happy. She sang all the time she was dusting and polishing and when Mr Evans complained, 'Tweet, tweet, tweet, do you think you're a bird, girl?' she actually answered him back. 'We're supposed to make a joyful noise unto the Lord, aren't we, Samuel?'

Carrie was sure he must guess something was up but he seemed less suspicious than usual, perhaps because he was happier. His son Frederick had written to say he was coming on leave and Mr Evans kept busy, tidying the shop and getting the books up to date. 'He'll see I haven't let things slide,' he said to Carrie, when she was helping him put the shelves straight. 'It'll give him heart, see? Knowing he's got a good sound business to come home to when this old War's over.'

Frederick came at the end of June, a broad, beefy soldier with a very big bottom. He looked very much like his father except that he was fatter, and red in the face where Mr Evans was pale. 'Snow White and Rose Red,' was what Carrie called them, but Nick had a better name. Frederick ate his meals with Mr Evans in the parlour and they were both fond of meat, liking it juicy and rare. Nick saw them one day when the door was left open, sitting with their elbows on the table and chewing their chops in their fingers. 'Blood running out of their mouths,' he told Carrie. 'They're Carnivores, that's what they are.'

Frederick was on leave for a week. He slept a lot of the time, either in bed or sprawled in the most comfortable chair in the kitchen and snoring loudly with his mouth open. The day before he left was a Saturday and

Nick and Carrie were going to spend it helping to harvest the small hay field at Druid's Bottom. 'Take Fred with you, why not?' Mr Evans said, when they were about to set off. 'Do him good to get off his backside for once!' Fred groaned in protest from his armchair and his father looked at him sharply. 'Might even do you some good in another direction, my lad! It's a long time since you've put in an appearance, isn't it? Paid your respects to your Auntie!'

Fred groaned again but sat up, quite good-humouredly, and put his boots on. 'Needs must when the old Devil drives,' he said, winking at Carrie when Mr Evans had gone. 'D'you mind if I come along?'

They did mind, but not very much. When he wasn't asleep, Frederick had been friendly enough, though he often laughed loudly for no reason they could see and said things there was no answer to, like 'Wotcha, young Carrie, how's tricks?' This sort of behaviour was tiresome but bearable and, as they walked to Druid's Grove, Carrie thought she quite liked him. He joked with them like a cheerful, older brother and sang one or two shockingly rude Army songs that made them both giggle. 'Mr Evans ought to hear you singing those songs, he'd have your hide, wouldn't he?' Nick said, and Frederick roared with laughter and swung him up on his shoulder and ran with him along the railway line as if he weighed nothing.

He was like a bear, Carrie thought: a friendly, silly, strong bear.

★

He was certainly stronger than anyone at Druid's Bottom. The hay had been cut a few days before and dried in the sun and Frederick made light work of heaving it up to Albert on the cart. Carrie and Nick and Mister Johnny helped too, to begin with, but their efforts were puny beside Frederick's and they tired much more quickly. Though the sweat poured down his red face his arms went on working like pistons and Albert barely had time to stack one great, whiskery load before another came up. He lurched from one side of the cart to the other, glasses flashing in the sun, his face pale and determined.

'Leelachalima,' Mister Johnny said, and put down his pitchfork.

Nick interpreted. 'He says, leave it to Fred and we might as well, really. Fred by himself is enough to wear Albert out.'

'Poor Albert,' Carrie said, thinking how shameful for him, not being able to keep up with Fred with all of them watching.

She had forgotten that Albert was never proud in that way. He heard what she said and shouted down to her. 'Help's what I want, not your pity. You stir your idle stumps, Carrie, and get up here with me! This isn't a *man* I've got pitching up hay to me, it's a flipping *machine*!'

It was lovely on the top of the cart. Carrie stood knee deep in the dry, sweet-smelling hay and helped Albert take Frederick's huge forkfuls that were so heavy, sometimes, it made them both stagger. They were glad to rest briefly, the sun warm on their backs, while Mister Johnny took the old horse's head and led the cart a little farther along. They were moving nearer the house all the time and by one o'clock they had finished the field. Carrie was hot and tired but wonderfully happy. She lay on her stomach on top of the hay, dusty spikes tickling her ears and her nostrils and said, 'I wish I was a farmer, I could go on harvesting for ever and ever and ever.'

'More than I could,' Albert said. 'I'm dead as a door nail. I don't think I'm constructed for physical labour. Is that Mr Evans's son you've got with you? Brawny chap, isn't he?'

'Not much brain though, I don't think,' Carrie said.

Frederick was leaning on his pitchfork, apparently listening to Mister Johnny who was waving his small hands and gabbling. Nick lay on the ground, watching them. It was all very peaceful: Mister Johnny's voice bubbling away like a lark and the sun on the hay field and on the tall-chimneyed house and on the quiet mountain behind it. Carrie's feeling of happiness grew until her bones seemed to ache with it. She yawned and stretched and said, 'This is the best place in the whole, wide world. In the whole *universe*. Don't you think so, Albert?'

Albert wasn't listening. He was kneeling up. 'Stop that,' he shouted. 'Stop it at once!'

Carrie looked where he looked. Frederick was dancing round Mister Johnny, twisting one side of his face in grotesque imitation and fluttering his hands.

'Gobble-gobble, gubble-gubble, tickledly pouffla ha!' he cried in a silly, mimicking voice, then laughed raucously and flipped Mister Johnny's bow tie undone.

Carrie heard Albert gasp beside her. Then – in the same second, it seemed – he was off the cart and racing towards them. But before he could get there Mister Johnny gave a high, piercing cry, quite unlike any sound Carrie had ever heard him make before, and flung himself on Frederick, arms flailing. Frederick stepped back, lost his balance, and went down like a tree falling. And Mister Johnny picked up a pitch-fork . . .

Carrie screamed and put her hands over her eyes. Shut away in panicky, red-spotted darkness, she heard Albert shout, 'Come on, Nick, help me hold him,' and then looked and saw Mister Johnny struggling between Albert and Nick, and Frederick crawling away, on the ground.

It was all over very quickly. By the time Carrie had jumped from the cart, Mister Johnny had stopped throwing himself about and had started to cry, his face screwed up and scarlet. The boys let him go and Nick found his handkerchief in his breast pocket and wiped his face and said gently, 'It's all right, Mister Johnny, all over now, let's go and find Hepzibah.' He took his hand and led him away and Mister Johnny went like a lamb.

Frederick was sitting up, white as chalk. 'Look,' he said, and Carrie saw the blood on his hand where the pitchfork had caught it.

She said, 'Serve you right. Serve you right if he'd *killed* you,' and he stared at her, his lower jaw drooping.

He said, 'He ought to be locked up, vicious loony like that,' and stood up. He walked as far as the cart, took a packet of cigarettes from his jacket that was hanging on the tailgate and stood, sullenly smoking.

Carrie said loudly, meaning him to hear her, 'What a foul, wicked beast!'

But Albert shook his head. 'Beast all right but stupid, not wicked. Just doesn't know how to treat someone like Mister Johnny. And he's not alone in that. Most people don't know, after all. They're either scared, or they laugh. Mister Johnny can't bear to be teased, *really* can't bear it! It sends him into a terrible rage. Hepzibah says when they lived in Norfolk she had an awful time looking after him because he was always in fights and he was young then, too young to hurt anyone much. It's been all right since they've lived here because so few people come. But Hepzibah says if they ever had to leave and go where there were strangers about who didn't understand his sensitive ways, then he might have to be – well – what *he* said!' He nodded at Frederick and said, in a low voice, 'Shut up in a madhouse, or something.'

'Mister Johnny's not mad!'

'No. At least, *I* don't think so. But you saw what he did, didn't you?' He pulled a helpless face, took off his glasses, and wiped them on the tail of his shirt.

Carrie said, 'See who's coming,' and he put them back on.

Mrs Gotobed was walking towards them, leaning on Hepzibah's arm. She wore a long, pale grey dress, trimmed with pink ostrich feathers round the hem. One thin, ring-studded hand held the skirt up at the front but the back went trail, trail, trail on the ground, sweeping up wisps of hay with the feathers. She was thinner than when Carrie had seen her before and had a transparent look, like a skeleton leaf: all her veins and bones showing. But her voice sounded strong as a bell. 'Well, Frederick, still playing the bully boy, are you?'

He came and stood in front of her. His expression was surprisingly meek. 'It was only a bit of a game, Auntie Dilys. A bit of a silly joke, see?'

'Silly's the right word. You always had a silly sense of humour, didn't you, Frederick?' Then she smiled though her eyes remained cold as winter and said, 'Are you enjoying your time in the Army?' – as if she were making conversation in the drawing-room, Carrie thought, instead of standing in a hay field in summer in a long, silk ball gown.

'Yes, Auntie Dilys.'

'And what will you do afterwards. When the war's over? Come back to the grocery shop?'

There was contempt in her tone, Carrie saw Frederick's neck redden. He said, 'No, I won't. That's one thing I'm fixed on. It's a narrow place, this valley, Auntie Dilys. Too narrow for me, I want something bigger.'

She looked him up and down. Then she said, 'It'll break your father's heart, I suppose you know that?'

Frederick didn't answer and she sighed a little. Then looked at Carrie.

She said, 'Well, Miss Emerald-Eyes? Enjoying yourself in my hay field?'

Carrie nodded. She was looking at Mrs Gotobed's dress. Pale grey silk with pink ostrich feathers. The one her husband had said made her look like a Queen. *I'm keeping that one till the last*, was what she'd told Carrie.

Carrie felt as if she were falling through space; falling and falling with the air pressing her chest and making her gasp. She dragged her gaze upwards but it was an effort: her eyelids seemed weighted with stones.

Mrs Gotobed's eyes were smiling at her; not cold now, but kind. As if she knew what Carrie was thinking and found it mildly amusing.

She said, 'Things are seldom as bad as you think they're going to be. Not when you come to them. So it's a waste of time, being afraid. You remember that!' She laughed softly, leaning on Hepzibah's arm, then went on, 'And remember the other thing, too. *Do* you remember? The message I gave you?'

'Yes,' Carrie said. 'Yes, I remember.'

*M*rs Gotobed died one hot day in July. Albert came to the shop in the late afternoon with a letter for Mr Evans from Hepzibah. He said, 'It happened this morning but there was no one to send till I came home from school.'

Mr Evans stood behind the counter and read the letter and Albert and Carrie watched him. He folded it neatly and put it back in its envelope and stared into space for a minute. Then he went to the front of the shop and pulled down the blinds. 'Respect for the dead,' he said, speaking to Carrie quite angrily, as if she had questioned this action. And went to the kitchen to tell Auntie Lou.

Carrie and Albert went up the mountain. Neither of them spoke as they climbed. Still without speaking, they sat on a hump of cropped grass, backs against a dry stone wall, the evening sun in their eyes. Carrie thought of all the people she knew in the world, all of them still eating and breathing and walking about, and then of Mrs Gotobed, lying still. Sweat stood cold on her forehead. She said, 'She's the first person I've ever known die, in my life.'

'She won't be the last, so you might as well get used to it,' Albert said – rather cruelly, it seemed.

'Do you have to speak like that?' Carrie said. 'In that *tone*?'

'No. But it was the way *you* spoke! This is the first sorrow of my life, poor little me!'

'I didn't mean that.'

'Didn't you?'

'No, I didn't.'

Albert poked a twig at a loose lump of earth. He lifted it and red ants scurried and bustled, pulling and pushing their torpedo-shaped eggs to safety. Within a few seconds they had all vanished into tiny, black holes. 'Amazing team work,' Albert said. 'What do you think *they* think happened?'

Carrie said, in a hurt, distant voice, 'Much what you'd think, I suppose, if someone took the roof off your house. Or a bomb blew it off.'

'People wouldn't act so fast, though. Not conditioned to it. They'd stop and think and wonder and while they were doing that someone's great boot would come down – *crump* – and that 'ud be the end of them . . .' He paused and looked shyly at Carrie. 'Sorry if I was beastly.'

'It's all right.'

'No, it isn't. I was upset and taking it out on you. That's a rotten trick.'

'It doesn't matter.'

'Yes, it *does*.'

They looked at each other and grinned. Carrie said, 'Did she – I mean, did it hurt her much? Dying?'

'Hepzibah said it was just like putting a light out at the end of a day.'

'Oh,' Carrie said. Then, 'What'll happen to Hepzibah? Will she have to leave Druid's Bottom? I mean, she's just the servant, she can't stay there, can she? Where will she go? And what'll happen to Mister Johnny? Oh, *Albert*!'

'Hang on, Tragedy Queen,' he said, 'it's all *right*. At least I suppose it will be because Mrs Gotobed told me. She said it would be a sin if they were turned out when she died, with Mister Johnny the way he is, and after Hepzibah had cared for her so well all these years. She said she was going to make a Will saying they could both stay on, without paying rent, as long as they wanted to. She couldn't leave them any money because all she had was an annuity that would come to an end when she died, but Mister Johnny's got a little bit that his parents left him and Hepzibah makes some from the poultry, so they should have just enough. Mrs Gotobed had worked it all out. She said she had no close relations to bother about on her husband's side and only the Evanses on hers. I think she's left her bits of jewellery to your Auntie Lou – there's not as much as you'd think, mostly glittery junk, paste copies of real stones. And the house to Mr Evans though it won't be much use to him. He can't sell it or let it, of course, while Hepzibah's living there.' He pulled a wry face. 'I expect he'll be flaming mad when he knows that, won't he? I expect he's counted on it. After all, he's her brother!'

'Her own flesh and blood. But sometimes you owe more to strangers,' Carrie said solemnly.

Albert stared at her and she laughed excitedly. 'That was what she told me to tell Mr Evans, once she was dead. That she'd done what she'd done – made this Will, that is – not to spite him but because it seemed the right thing. And the Right Thing was to take care of Mister Johnny and Hepzibah Green. I didn't understand what she meant at the time, I just thought she was mad!'

Now she did understand, it seemed beautiful, even if sad. Although they had quarrelled so bitterly Mrs Gotobed had still loved Mr Evans, deep down in her heart, and the message she had asked Carrie to give him would show him this plain. 'Oh,' Carrie said, 'it'll make him so happy.'

'I wouldn't be too sure of that,' Albert said.

'But it *will*,' Carrie cried. 'Don't you see? He worried about her all the time, he was even jealous of Hepzibah because she was looking after her and he wasn't! So he'll be glad to know that she thought about *him* and wanted him to know it.'

The way Albert was staring at her, dry and disbelieving with one eyebrow raised, was so maddening! 'Of course you wouldn't understand,' Carrie said. 'You haven't got a brother or sister so you just don't *know*, do you, how someone might feel! I know how I would, because I've got Nick. If we'd not spoken to each other for years and he died it would make all the difference to have someone say he was still fond of me. I expect it'll make all the difference to poor Mr Evans.' She thought of him, of how he must feel now, mourning his dead sister and wishing he had had some last word from her; and then, how she would give him Mrs Gotobed's message, to comfort him. She thought of a beautiful phrase – *to comfort his sad heart* – and tears came into her eyes. 'I expect he'll just weep for joy when I tell him,' she said.

'Well, if you say so,' Albert said doubtfully. 'Though if I were you, I wouldn't be in *too* much of a hurry.'

But Carrie couldn't wait. Good news couldn't wait. She told him the first chance she had, when they had had tea and he was eating his lonely meal in the parlour.

She said, 'Mr Evans, I've got something to tell you, something important,' and then rushed straight into it before he could stop her and say, 'Clear out while I'm eating.' She told him what Mrs Gotobed had asked her to tell him, her exact words, and then explained what she was sure she had meant. Mr Evans listened in bulging-eyed silence, and when he still didn't speak, even when she had finished, she thought he hadn't taken it in.

She said, 'So you see, she *did* think of you, and wanted you to know that she had. I didn't understand what she meant about sometimes you owe more to strangers, but I do now. She meant Hepzibah and Mister Johnny and how she owed it to them to let them stay in the house because there was nowhere else they *could* go, not with Mister Johnny's shy ways. And of course she knew you wouldn't *mind*. I mean, I expect she knew how you felt about the only things worth having being the things you'd worked hard for and earned for *yourself*, so you wouldn't want her to leave you the house! But she didn't want you to think she'd forgotten you, or that she was just being spiteful, or something . . .'

'I knew it,' he said. His eyes bulged as if they were coming out of his head. '*I knew it.*'

'Of course you did,' Carrie said kindly. 'I suppose I'd know, really, if it was Nick and me. Even if we hadn't seen each other for ages and ages. I'd know he was still fond of me because I'm his sister. But it would be nice to be told that he was all the same, even if it did make me feel a bit sad.'

'Sad?' he repeated wonderingly. '*Sad?*' As if this was some peculiar new word he'd not heard before.

'Well, a *bit*,' Carrie said. 'Only in a nice way, of course.'

He said nothing. The silence grew and grew. Carrie tried to think of some way to break it.

At last she said slowly, 'What I mean is, looking back over the past is always a bit sad, even if what you're remembering is happy times, because it's over and done. Like if Nick was dead and I was remembering the things we'd done *this* year, perhaps. Living here with you and Auntie Lou, and going to Druid's Bottom, and getting the hay in, and listening to Hepzibah's stories. Only of course I can't really imagine Nick dying . . .'

But thinking of it, thinking of Nick being dead and herself being lonely without him, made her eyes start to swim. When Mr Evans stood up his face wobbled in front of her.

He said, in a terrible voice, 'Hepzibah, Hepzibah, *Hepzibah*! So she's got at you too, has she? Bewitched you with her lying tales and slippery ways as well as my poor sister!'

He pushed roughly past her and out of the room. He roared down the passage, 'Louisa, LOUISA . . .'

He had knocked over the water jug when he got up from the table. Carrie tried to mop up the mess with the edge of the tablecloth and put a mat under the worst of it to stop the damp marking the table, but her hands seemed all thumbs and she couldn't stop crying. It had all gone wrong somehow; she didn't know why, but it had. Mr Evans was angry and he shouldn't have been, she had tried so hard to explain . . .

Nick said, beside her, 'What on earth have you done?'

'T'wasn't me,' she sobbed. 'It was him. *He* knocked the jug over.'

'I didn't mean that, you half-witted dope! Just listen to him. Did you start him off?'

He was shouting at Auntie Lou in the kitchen. '. . . told you what was going on, didn't I? Told you she'd got her claws in, but you wouldn't have it. Miss Green this, Miss Green that! So kind to poor Dilys! Oh, there's kind she's been! She knew what she was doing, that snake in the grass, that viper! And I daresay she thinks she's succeeded – done me out of my rights and fixed up a snug home for herself for the rest of her days! But I shan't let it lie, she needn't think it. Not if I have to drag her through every court in the land . . .'

Nick closed the parlour door. He whispered, half scared, half excited. 'Whatever did you say to him, Carrie?'

'Nothing wrong, I don't think. I don't know.' She mopped her eyes with the tablecloth but it was too wet to help much. 'I just told him something Mrs Gotobed asked me to tell him. I thought he'd be pleased. Perhaps he would have been, if I'd explained properly. But I did try! I said how I'd feel if it was you and me, and we'd quarrelled, and you'd died . . .'

Nick gawped at her. 'You're potty. Quite potty! He'll have you locked up, I should think!'

'I was only trying to put myself in his place,' Carrie said. 'I felt sorry for him.'

'Then you really are nutty as a fruit cake,' Nick said with conviction.

CHAPTER 11

Mr Evans's rages were noisy while they lasted but they didn't last long. Nick and Carrie were used to timing them now, fairly accurately: they went out for about half an hour and when they came back he was sitting quiet in the kitchen, reading the paper. He looked up in a thoughtful way that made Carrie nervous but all he said was, 'Well, Carrie, I'm much obliged to you! Out of the mouths of babes and sucklings!' It seemed an odd remark but he made it quite amiably and Carrie's immediate reaction was one of relief: at least he wasn't angry with her!

He had been angry with Hepzibah, though, and

thinking about it, lying awake in bed that night, and at
school the next day, Carrie knew she must warn her.
Albert had said Mr Evans would be flaming mad when
he heard about Mrs Gotobed's Will and it seemed
Albert was right. Mr Evans *was* flaming mad, not with
Mrs Gotobed but with Hepzibah for 'doing him out of
his rights'. He had said he would drag her through
every court in the land, which sounded unpleasantly
threatening. And if he did something dreadful to Hepzibah it would be all Carrie's fault, though she hadn't
meant any harm, only passed on a message. But when
she thought about it an odd picture came into her head;
a picture of herself innocently lifting the lid of a box
and letting out a dark, shapeless shadow . . .

All day this shadow grew in her mind and by the
time school was over and she was running along the
railway line, it seemed to be running behind her like
some dark, winged creature. She ran faster and faster,
afraid to look back, but with hope in her heart. She
would be safe once she reached Hepzibah's kitchen . . .

But Mr Evans had been there before her . . .

She knew it at once. There was nothing obviously
wrong – Albert sitting at one end of the table in front
of his books and Hepzibah making an apple pie at the
other, pressing the pastry top with a fork to make a
frill round the edge – but it was as if a light had gone out.
From the room, from their faces . . .

Albert said, 'We've had a visitor, Carrie.' His expression was stony and she knew that he blamed her.

Hepzibah said, 'Only natural that he should want to come and pay his last respects to his sister.'

'Poking about among her things. That's what he came to do,' Albert said.

Hepzibah sighed. 'Her next-of-kin, Albert. Within his rights there.'

Albert said – and it was like a cold statue speaking – 'And to tell you to clear out, Hepzibah! Was *that* within his rights, too?'

She answered, quite calmly, 'A month's notice is reasonable. Gives me time to find somewhere. It shouldn't be difficult, there's plenty of farms could do with a bit of help with men away at the war. We only want two rooms and our keep and I've got a strong back and I'm willing. So's Mister Johnny, in his own way. He's good with cows and with sheep, lambing time.'

Carrie burst out, 'But, Albert! You said they could stay here?'

'I was wrong, it seems.'

'But you *told* me . . .'

'And you told *him*, didn't you?'

Hepzibah said, 'That's enough, Albert!' She smiled faintly at Carrie. 'There's no Will and that's that! Mr Evans rang the Bank and her London solicitors and there's no sign of one anywhere. I expect the poor soul took the will for the deed, if you'll excuse a weak joke. She had a kind thought and she believed she'd carried it through, and that's not uncommon, with someone as sick as she was and in pain a lot of the time. So there's no call to blame her.'

'Oh, I don't blame *her*,' Albert said.

Hepzibah looked at them both. Then she put the apple pie into the range oven and slammed the door so hard that coals fell into the grate. She riddled the dust and made up the fire and said, 'You two make friends time that's cooked. Or you'll get the rough edge of my tongue. I'm short on patience this evening.'

Albert stood up and jerked his head at Carrie. 'Come on, you. Do what she tells you.'

Carrie followed him out of the kitchen, through the hall, and up the polished stairs. A door stood ajar on the landing and Carrie saw the bottom end of a silk-covered bed and drawn, silken curtains. Mrs Gotobed's bedroom!

She stood still, heart hammering. '*Is she in there?*'

Albert's face was contemptuous. 'Couldn't hurt you if she was, but she isn't, she's downstairs, in her coffin. It's not *her* I wanted to show you.'

He pushed the door wide. The big, dim room smelt of roses. Carrie saw a big bowl of them on a table and then their reflection – and hers – in what seemed hundreds of mirrors. They covered the walls; when Albert opened the cupboard doors to show her Mrs Gotobed's wardrobe, the whole room became a shimmering rainbow of colour.

'Her dresses,' Albert whispered. 'All her dresses.'

'Twenty-nine,' Carrie said. 'One for each year of her marriage.'

Albert blinked; caught his breath. Then he recovered and spoke with a cold, held-in anger. 'Your Mr Evans!

Do you know what he did? He came up here and he went through them all, counted them, and wrote down the number. Then he told Hepzibah he'd hold her responsible! As if he thought she might steal them! Hepzibah didn't say what else he said but I don't suppose, taking *that* for a guide, it was exactly friendly, do you?'

Carrie shook her head. *That viper, that snake in the grass!* Had he said that to Hepzibah?

'Went through her drawers too, I dare say,' Albert said. '*And* her jewel box!'

It stood on the dressing table, among silver-topped bottles. A shining, ebony box, its lid open, showing a tray lined with blue velvet. Jewels winked up, like bright eyes.

Albert was frowning. He stood straight and still, breathing hard as if he were stealing himself to do something. Carrie waited, but when he moved all he did was to lift the tray out of the box. There was a cavity beneath with a string of pearls in it.

Albert said slowly, 'Oh, well. It was just a chance, I suppose . . .'

'Chance of what?' Carrie asked but Albert didn't reply because Mister Johnny suddenly spoke from the doorway.

'Geelalookala, geelalookala . . .' He scurried into the room and came up to them, smiling hopefully into their faces. 'Geelalookala, *geelalookala* . . .' He wasn't talking as he sometimes did, just for the sake of making a conversational noise. He was trying to tell them something.

Albert looked at him intently. He said, in an urgent voice, 'Try, Mister Johnny. Please try harder.'

Mister Johnny's smile vanished and he screwed up his face and puckered his mouth but all that came out was a string of indecipherable, watery sounds.

Albert sighed.

Mister Johnny was watching his face. He said, 'Schlakali.' He started to laugh excitedly, put his little hand into the jewel box, took it out again, and touched his breast pocket. Then he put his head on one side and looked at Albert in an expectant way, like a dog waiting to be given a biscuit.

'I wonder,' Albert said. 'I wonder . . .'

Mr Johnny was making a queer, sucking sound with his lips. It seemed familiar to Carrie. 'Mr Evans does that! His false teeth are loose. Nick says he's too mean to buy new ones.'

'I think that's it!' Albert said. 'Mr Evans was in here and he took something out of the jewel box. Is that what you're trying to say, Mister Johnny?'

But Mister Johnny just laughed; he was bored with this game. He wandered off round the room, looking at himself in the mirrors and pulling faces and laughing.

Albert said, 'I'm sure he did see Mr Evans and I think what he saw him take was an envelope. I saw one in the box once when she was trying her pearls on to see if they went with one of the dresses. A brown envelope. I'm quite sure I saw it, I've got a sort of picture in my mind's eye. Not that I thought much about it, why should I? Until Hepzibah said there wasn't a Will anywhere. Then I thought, well, perhaps that was it!'

'But there isn't a Will,' Carrie said. 'Mr Evans rang the solicitors, didn't he?'

'In London.' Albert took off his glasses and rubbed them on his handkerchief and put them back on, as if clean spectacles might make him think better. Then he said, speaking softly and half to himself, 'Suppose she got someone local to make a Will for her and then kept it here? To go through it sometimes and change it – old people like to do that. Hepzibah says she knew an old woman once who kept what she called a Death Book. With what she was going to leave to each of her relations written down in it so that when she got fed up with one of them she could just strike his name out!'

'What a beastly idea,' Carrie said. 'But it's nothing to do with what we're talking about, is it? I mean, Mr Evans wouldn't take Mrs Gotobed's *Will*. Why should he do that?'

'God give me strength!' Albert raised his eyes to heaven. 'Carrie, you innocent *nit*! If a person dies intestate – that's without making a Will – then everything they've got to leave goes to their nearest relations. Mr Evans and Auntie Lou, in this case. The house'll go to them, and the jewels, and her dresses. Nothing to Hepzibah, not even the right to stay on here. So all Mr Evans had to do, to get rid of her, was take the Will and destroy it!'

'But that would be terribly wrong!' Carrie cried.

'Clever girl.'

'I don't believe he would do it. I just don't *believe* it.'

Albert grinned at her in an indulgent, knowing way and it made her angry.

'If *you* believe he did it, then you can do something about it, can't you, Mr Fancy-Yourself? Tell someone . . .'

Albert stopped grinning. 'Oh yes? And who'd listen? To a fourteen-year-old boy who *thinks* he saw an envelope in a box once, and an idiot who can't even say what he saw?'

Carrie was so shocked to hear him call Mister Johnny an idiot that she couldn't speak, only stare. Albert's eyes fell, and he blushed.

He muttered, 'Oh, it's so stupid! If only I'd looked earlier on! I could have looked last night, if I'd thought. But even if I'd *thought*, it wouldn't have seemed right to go poking and prying with her only just dead. Hepzibah wouldn't have liked it. She'd have said it wasn't respectful.' He sighed, very deeply, and looked at Carrie. 'I would have looked in the end, though. Tonight, I expect, or tomorrow. And that would have been time enough if you hadn't shot your mouth off and brought that foul man roaring round here . . .'

Carrie gasped. 'That's not *fair*.'

'No. No, it isn't. But fairness doesn't come into it really. I mean, me being fair to you. If I wasn't, I'm sorry, but it isn't important. What is important is that Hepzibah's got to leave Druid's Bottom. And of course she'll say it's all right and she'll manage but she's just being brave.' He stopped and went on in a low voice, 'I came back early from school and when I came in I saw she'd been crying.'

'*Hepzibah?*'

'She said she'd been peeling onions. But I could tell because her mouth looked all slippery. Onions just make your eyes water.'

Carrie said, 'Suppose – suppose she *asked* Mr Evans? To let them stay – well, not for ever, but for more than a month. Till the war's over, perhaps.' That seemed, when she thought about it, almost as good as saying for ever.

'Too proud,' Albert said. 'Besides, it wouldn't be any use, would it? He wouldn't budge.'

'She could put a spell on him,' Carrie said.

Albert smiled at her but so sadly that it brought her no comfort. Even if they were friends again, perhaps he still blamed her, secretly. Perhaps Hepzibah blamed her . . .

She left Albert with Mister Johnny and went downstairs to the kitchen. Hepzibah was darning socks. She looked up at Carrie and smiled.

Carrie stood by her chair. She said, 'Hepzibah . . .'

She didn't know what else to say, but there was no need to say anything. Hepzibah's brilliant eyes looked into hers and Carrie felt as if something inside her, some hard, painful lump, were dissolving. She started to cry with happy relief and Hepzibah put her mending aside and took her on to her lap as if she were Nick.

She said, 'Hush. Hush, my lambkin,' and rocked her a little, and then, when Carrie was quiet, 'I should think that old pie's nearly ready. Wait till I've cut it and we're all sat down with a piece, and I'll tell you a story.'

And when Albert and Mister Johnny came in, she cut the pie and told them about the big fair that was held every Michaelmas in the Norfolk village where she had lived when she was a little girl; about the gay gipsy carts and the fire eater, and the booth where you could have a tooth pulled for sixpence with a brass band to drown your screams; about the two-headed calf and the Bearded Lady and the Toffee Woman. 'She was a fine, big woman with hair black as night,' Hepzibah said. 'And you never tasted such toffee! It made your mouth water even though you'd seen how it was made! She'd pick up a great lump of it and throw it over a nail and then oil her hands with spit and draw it out and out in a long skein, till it was smooth as glass . . .'

Mister Johnny sat quiet and still as he always did when she talked, watching her mouth and moving his own as if he were trying to copy her. Albert sat, hugging his knees, and staring at nothing. He had a bit of a beak for a nose and in profile, especially when he was frowning and thoughtful, looked like a young, dreaming hawk. Carrie knew that although he was soothed, as she was, by the sound of Hepzibah's voice, he was not really listening. She leaned against Hepzibah's knee and watched Albert and wondered what he was plotting.

CHAPTER 12

*M*r Evans and Auntie Lou went to Mrs Gotobed's funeral. When they came back Auntie Lou was red-eyed but Mr Evans seemed almost cheerful. 'Well, that's over,' he said, and went straight upstairs to change out of his good suit.

Carrie had been minding the shop. It was the first time she had been left on her own and she had managed quite well except that she had given Mrs Prichard, the colliery manager's wife, short change by mistake. Only sixpence, but Mr Evans sent her off to return it at once. Whatever else was wrong with him he was at least *honest*, Carrie thought as she ran up the town. The idea of him stealing Mrs Gotobed's Will was a bit of what Hepzibah would call 'Albert's Old Nonsense'.

But Carrie brooded about it all the same. The summer holidays had begun and she had plenty of time to spend in the shop, helping Mr Evans and watching him and wondering . . . He was a bully, he flew into rages, but to do what Albert believed he had done he would have to be wicked, and Carrie didn't think he was that. He was even kind sometimes, letting old age pensioners have credit if they were short at the end of the week, and once he sent a box of free groceries to a poor woman whose husband had died of pneumonia. 'It's the Lord's will we should take care of the Widows and Orphans,' he said.

Hepzibah and Mister Johnny were not exactly widows and orphans of course but perhaps, Carrie thought, Mr Evans could be persuaded to think it was the Lord's will to help them as well. If she were him she would want to, but she knew now that it was no use trying to put herself in his place. She had thought he would be happy about Mrs Gotobed's message because *she* would have been, but she had been wrong about that. He had simply been angry and believed that it meant he had been right all the time and that his sister really was in Hepzibah's Power. That Hepzibah had bewitched Mrs Gotobed . . .

Did Mr Evans really believe that Hepzibah was a witch? Religious people didn't believe in witches and Mr Evans was very religious. Carrie wondered if *she* believed it and decided she wasn't quite sure. Hepzibah was good at most things she did, making pastry and telling stories and keeping poultry. If she was a witch she would be good at that, too. Her magic would have worked. Mrs Gotobed would have made a Will and Hepzibah and Mister Johnny would be safe in Druid's Bottom for ever and ever . . .

But Albert was so sure that she *had* made a Will . . .

Carrie's head seemed to spin like a top. So many thoughts twisting round, it made her quite giddy. Tired, too: she lay awake at night, thinking, and came down several mornings so pale that Auntie Lou wanted to go to the chemist and buy her a tonic.

'Waste of good money,' Mr Evans said. 'Stewing indoors, that's the trouble. Bit of exercise and fresh air, that's all you need, girl! Get your bowels moving . . .' Speaking crossly and rudely although Carrie had only been stewing indoors because she had been helping him in the shop! His unfairness gave her something else to brood over. Mr Evans was unfair. *Life* was unfair. Poor Hepzibah and poor Mister Johnny. Poor Carrie and Nick, having to live here with this rude, unfair man for the rest of the war. For the rest of their lives, probably . . .

But they were not even to stay for the rest of that year. A letter came from their mother. She had resigned from her ambulance unit because her own mother was ill and had rented a house outside Glasgow so that she could look after her and still be near the port when their father's ship came in. It was a small house, only a cottage, but there was an attic room for the children and a good school not too far away. She was sending Auntie Lou the money for their rail tickets and they were to leave in two weeks' time. She wrote, 'That's not long, is it? I'm so happy, my darlings.'

Carrie didn't know if she was happy or not. It was all so sudden it made her feel queer; affecting her stomach like looking down from the top of a cliff or riding on a Big Dipper.

Nick actually grumbled. 'I don't want to go to rotten old Glasgow. I don't want to go to a new school. I don't want to leave Auntie Lou.'

He and Auntie Lou were thick as thieves at the moment. Several times, Carrie had come into the kitchen and found them giggling together. 'It's a secret,' Nick said when she asked him what they were laughing about. 'You're Mr Evans's friend. Helping him all the time. I'm Auntie Lou's.'

'Keep your silly old secret,' Carrie said. 'Fat lot I care!'

But she felt a bit bruised. Suddenly it seemed she had no one to talk to. Nick had said he didn't want to leave Auntie Lou but as soon as he was used to the idea, he was over the moon with excitement. Singing made-up songs all the time about living in Scotland and seeing their mother, while Carrie still felt nothing much, one way or the other.

She went to Druid's Bottom but she felt tongue-tied there. Hepzibah smiled and was friendly but there was no life in her face – like a pond with a thin skim of ice,

Carrie thought. Even Mister Johnny was quiet, sitting in a corner of the kitchen, just watching Hepzibah, and Albert was unusually silent. Not as if he were angry with Carrie but as if he were busy thinking his own thoughts . . .

When she told them about her mother's letter he simply nodded, as if their going away wasn't important. He would have to go away himself, leaving Druid's Bottom when Hepzibah left, although he wasn't leaving the valley. He was to stay with Mr Morgan, the Minister.

'Will you like that?' Carrie asked timidly, and he just shrugged his shoulders.

Hepzibah looked at Carrie's woebegone face. She said, 'We'll all be pulling up sticks about the same time, then! I tell you what we'll do, we'll have a joint farewell party! Now take that look off your faces, Mr Misery and Miss Gloom, and go and collect the eggs for me, will you? Mister Johnny's not feeling up to the mark at the moment.'

'He's not ill, just scared stiff,' Albert said as they went into the yard. 'Won't leave Hepzibah alone for a minute. He doesn't understand, I suppose, and that makes it worse because he feels *more*. Things coming to an end.'

He picked up a stone and flung it into the horse pond. They watched the ripples spread.

'How deep is it?' Carrie asked.

'Bottomless. No, that's nonsense, of course, it can't be.' He sighed and squared his shoulders. 'Come on, let's get on with it.'

They collected the eggs. There was no fun in it. Carrie said, 'All the poultry, that's Hepzibah's, isn't it? And the cow belongs to Mister Johnny. What'll happen to them?'

'They'll be sold, I suppose. The cow and the horse and the geese, anyway. There's one farm where they might take the hens, but Hepzibah didn't seem keen on it. The farmer didn't actually refuse to take Mister Johnny but he made it clear he didn't really want him. He said he might frighten his wife, or the children, or something.'

'They mustn't go there, then!'

'Depends what else turns up, doesn't it? Beggars can't be choosers. They've got to go somewhere.'

'Unless . . .' Carrie looked at him sideways. 'I did think I might ask Mr Evans if they could stay on here. But I only *thought*, so it's no good. I didn't *do* it.'

'Not when it came to it,' Albert said. 'Same thing happened to me.'

'Do you mean *you* were going to ask Mr Evans?'

'Not that. But I thought . . .' He glanced at Carrie and then said, very quickly, 'If I tell you, don't laugh.'

'No,' Carrie promised and remembered she had once said 'Don't laugh' to him. When they were walking up through the Grove on her birthday. It seemed years ago now.

Albert's face was solemn and growing pink. 'It's just that I thought you shouldn't be able to turn people out of places they've lived in for years, it doesn't make *sense*. So I thought, there might be a Law about it, and the best thing to do would be to ask a solicitor. I could say Mrs Gotobed had made a Will but we couldn't find it. I thought if I told him that he'd be bound to make a proper search – not in the house, I don't mean, I've looked in the house – but among other solicitors she might have gone to. They'd have a record if she *had* made a Will. So I went to see Mr Rhys. The solicitor in War Memorial Square.'

He stopped. Carrie looked at him and waited. Albert sighed. 'I didn't get any farther than his waiting room. I sat there for about ten minutes and then I came out. I knew it wasn't any use. I mean, what would you do if you were a lawyer and a boy came in and started yapping on about missing Wills like in some kid's story? I could just hear Mr Rhys saying, *Run away, little man, back to your comics!* And even if that didn't happen, even if he listened and said he'd do something, it wouldn't be any good because Hepzibah wouldn't have any part in it. Can you see her, going to law?'

Carrie said, 'I'll not stay where I'm not wanted so you needn't think it!' mimicking Hepzibah in a determined mood, and Albert laughed briefly. Carrie said, 'I think, all the same, once I got there I'd have *told* him.'

'I believe you would,' Albert said. 'But that's you, not me, isn't it? Once you've made up your mind to something I think you usually do it. I'm not like that. Trouble is, I start *thinking*. That there's no point, that sort of thing. If you'd been with me, I might have stiffened myself and gone on with it. But you never believed in her Will, did you? So I couldn't ask you to come . . .'

'That's *mean*,' Carrie said. 'That's really mean, Albert Sandwich!'

He nodded shamefaced. 'Yes, it is. I'm just making excuses. And picking on you because you're not a rotten coward like I am. *That's* the only reason I slunk out of that place! I was scared that he'd laugh at me!'

He looked so miserable. Carrie said generously, 'You're not a coward, stupid!'

'Yes, I am.'

'No, you're not. You're just – just too clever to rush into things.'

Albert closed his eyes and moaned, 'Oh, I hate myself!' Then he opened them and kicked savagely at a lump of dried mud, sending it sailing across the yard to explode against the side of the stable. He said, 'No, that's not true, I don't hate myself, what's the point? But I know what I *am* and I don't like it much. I'm quite clever but I'm not at all brave.' He looked at her and grinned suddenly. 'I suppose I might as well get used to it.'

Carrie thought of something to comfort him. 'It wouldn't have helped being brave. Mr Rhys wouldn't have paid any attention. Grown-ups only listen to grown-ups.'

'I wish I was grown-up,' Albert said. 'It's a fearful *handicap* being a child. You have to stand there and watch, you can never make anything happen. Or stop things you don't like. If I was grown-up, I could stop *this*. I could look after Hepzibah, I could buy Druid's Bottom, and we could all live there together. You and Nick, too. Though I suppose you'd rather go to Scotland and be with your mother.'

'Not specially,' Carrie said. 'I mean, I do want to go, in a way, but in another way I'd rather stay here. I wish there was two of me, really. I feel *torn* in two.'

CHAPTER 13

*T*he days flew by on wings. Two weeks seemed *so* long to begin with, but there was so much to do. So many Last Things.

Nick made up songs about them. The Last Time on the slag heap, bumping face down on the old tray and scraping his knee. The Last Time at Chapel. The Last Time making a dam in the stream at the end of the garden.

He was so happy that Carrie was afraid Auntie Lou might be hurt but she didn't appear to be. She joined in Nick's songs and was as silly as he was, bright-eyed and laughing at nothing.

Only Mr Evans seemed to share Carrie's queer, sinking feeling of sadness. 'I'm going to miss my assistant,' he said, more than once. 'You've been a real help to me, Carrie.'

And this rare compliment made Carrie feel sadder still each time she heard it.

The Last Day . . .

The night before, their suitcases were packed and waiting. Auntie Lou had washed all their clothes, darned all the holes. The range fire was stoked so they could have a Last Bath.

Mr Evans said, 'Tomorrow dinner time, we'll have a picnic.'

Carrie and Nick couldn't believe it. Surprise made Nick giggle. He put his hand over his mouth and Auntie Lou shot a warning glance at him.

Carrie thought it was partly because they were going to have a farewell tea at Druid's Bottom. When she had told Mr Evans, he had gone very quiet; and then, just as they were going up for their bath, he suggested the picnic. 'A Last Treat, see?'

Auntie Lou had a basket packed with sausage rolls, cheese sandwiches and firm, greenish tomatoes. It was an extraordinary sight to see Mr Evans shutting the shop in the middle of the day and toiling up the mountain like an ordinary person. He sweated a lot because he wasn't accustomed to climbing. 'Used to come up here quite a lot when I was a lad,' he said, mopping his forehead. 'Seems to have got steeper since!'

While Auntie Lou set out the food, he sat on a flat rock to recover and talked about the old days. 'Used to carry your Auntie up here when I was a young man and she was a babby,' he said. 'I'd set her down here and dare her to move while I tickled trout in that stream. D'you remember that, girl?'

Auntie Lou nodded; then blushed, for some reason. She was oddly quiet, seemed in an odd mood altogether, though not an unhappy one: while they were eating she sat staring over the valley with a dreamy look in her eyes and a small, secret smile on her face. Mr Evans's voice boomed on about the things he had done when he was a boy – mostly earning money in his spare time to help his poor mother – but though Auntie Lou seemed to be listening, she wasn't listening to him. It was as if she were holding a much more exciting conversation inside her own head, Carrie decided.

As soon as lunch was over, Mr Evans was fidgeting to get back to the shop. 'Hurry up, young Nick, help Auntie Lou with the basket, jump to it double-quick now! Some of us have to work for our living, I'd never have got anywhere if I'd moved at your pace!' And when they got back he put on his working jacket with a sigh of relief and said, 'Well, that's over.'

Nick said, dutifully, 'Thank you, Mr Evans.'

Carrie said, 'It was lovely. A lovely picnic.'

'Well, as long as you enjoyed it,' he said – as if *he* hadn't, at all – but he looked pleased, all the same. And then, curiously shy. He took two small parcels out of his pocket. 'Might as well have these now, mightn't you? I've got a Council Meeting this evening. You'll be fast asleep time I get back.'

A knife for Nick, a marvellous knife in a sheath of green leather, and a small ring for Carrie. A real gold ring with a small dark red stone.

'Oh,' Nick said. '*Oh!* I've always wanted a sheath knife. I mean, the penknife you gave me for Christmas was very nice but it doesn't cut things. This is just what I wanted, it's my very best thing!'

'Take care of it, then,' Mr Evans said. He looked at Carrie.

'The ring's beautiful,' she said. She couldn't say 'Thank you,' the words stuck in her throat, but Mr Evans seemed to know how she felt.

'As long as you're pleased. Just a keepsake to remember us by. From your Auntie too, mind!'

It was easier to thank Auntie Lou. 'Thank you so much,' Carrie said, and Auntie Lou blushed and smiled. There were tears in her eyes and when they went through to the kitchen she hugged and kissed them both. She said, 'Oh, there's happy I've been with you two, there's been life in this house, first time I've known it!'

Nick flung his arms round her. 'Good-bye, Auntie Lou. I do love you.' He squeezed her so hard that she gasped, and for so long that Carrie grew restless. 'Do give over,' she said. 'You'll see Auntie Lou again, it's not the Last Time for that!'

★

'Last time on the railway line,' Nick sang. 'Last time *walking* along the railway line because tomorrow we'll go in the train, *puff-puff*, we'll go in the train and *screech-whistle-screech* . . .'

'Do be quiet,' Carrie said.

Nick pulled a face and walked beside her. 'Will we be bombed in Glasgow? Will the train be bombed on the way?'

'Of course not.' Carrie thought of bombs falling, of the war going on all this year they'd been safe in the valley; going on over their heads like grown-up conversation when she'd been too small to listen. She said, 'Don't be scared, Nick. Mum wouldn't send for us if it wasn't safe. Don't be scared anyway. I'll be with you.'

'I'm not scared, I'd like to be bombed, it 'ud be super exciting!' He started to sing again. 'Bomb, *bomb*, bang, *shee-ow*, ack, ack, ack . . .' Spreading out his arms and pretending to be an aeroplane, flying low, machine-gunning.

'Shut up, you bloodthirsty boy, you're spoiling it all,' Carrie said. 'Let's have *one* Last Time in peace and quiet!'

The Farewell Tea was spread in Hepzibah's kitchen: cold chicken and salad, a cheese and onion pie, a big plate of drop scones, thickly buttered. The range fire was glowing, hot enough to roast anyone who stood close to it. The back door stood open to let out the heat and Hepzibah's chickens wandered in and out, pecking at crumbs and sleepily chortling.

Nick stuffed and stuffed as if he hadn't seen food for weeks but Carrie could hardly eat anything. It was all ending so beautifully: the picnic and Mr Evans being so nice, and the ring and the knife, and now this last, lovely tea, with faces she loved round the table. She was so full, so tight with happiness, she felt she would burst if she ate one more drop scone.

Hepzibah wasn't eating much either. Once or twice she met Carrie's eye and smiled as if to say she felt just as she did. She cut Nick a fourth slice of pie and said, 'What a boy! When the Last Trump sounds, the first thing he'll say when he pops his head out of his grave will be *where's my breakfast?*'

'Our mother says she doesn't know where he puts it all, he's so thin,' Carrie said, and as soon as she had spoken it struck her that she had never talked to them about her mother before.

'What's your mother like?' Albert asked.

'Well, she's quite tall,' Carrie began, and then stopped. Not because she couldn't remember, but because it was such a long time since she'd seen her and she felt strange, suddenly, knowing that this time tomorrow they would be on their way to Scotland and she would be waiting for them. She thought, suppose I don't recognize her, suppose she doesn't recognize *me*, and felt her face grow hot.

'She's got blue eyes like mine,' Nick said. 'Navy blue eyes. That's why our father married her, because he's in the Navy. But she's not as pretty as you, Hepzibah. And she can't cook nearly as well. That's the best cheese and onion pie I've ever had in my whole life, and cheese and onion pie is my best thing.'

'And the last for now, Mr Cupboard-Love,' Hepzibah said. 'No more, not one crumb, or you'll be sick on the journey tomorrow.'

'He was sick when we came,' Carrie said.

'I was not!'

'Yes, you were. And it was all your own fault because you were stinking pig greedy and ate all my chocolate.'

'Stinking pig greedy yourself!'

'Sssala. Ssschalala,' Mister Johnny said. It was the first thing he'd said, all afternoon. He had got down from the table half-way through tea and was sitting on a chair in the doorway, looking droopy and listless.

'That's right, Mister Johnny,' Hepzibah said. 'Hush now, the pair of you.'

'I'll hush if you'll tell us a story.' Nick went to Hepzibah and leaned on her knee. 'I'm worn out with eating,' he said, 'I want to sit on your lap while you tell us a story.'

Hepzibah heaved him up, pretending to groan with his weight. 'Which one do you want then, Mr Big-Baby? You've heard them all, haven't you?'

Nick sighed and wriggled comfortably. 'The one about the poor African boy.'

'What made you think of that foolish tale?'

'Mister Johnny's playing with the skull,' Albert said.

He was stroking it. He had the skull half hidden in his lap and his little hand stroked the smooth bone, gently and rhythmically. Carrie had often seen him sit like that, fondling one of Hepzibah's chickens.

Hepzibah said, 'Put that down, Mister Johnny! This minute!'

The children had never heard her speak to him sharply before. They stared in surprise and she said in a tired voice, 'Oh, it doesn't matter, I suppose, not the old skull, but he's run me ragged just lately, picking up things round the house and putting them down where they shouldn't be. He had the silver this morning – all the best spoons, out in the yard!'

'You'd just polished them,' Albert said. 'It was the shine that attracted him, you know he's like a magpie that way. He was only making patterns with the spoons, you've never minded before.'

'Things are different now, aren't they?' Hepzibah said. 'I don't want Mr Evans to find anything missing.'

'He'd hardly make a fuss about an old skull,' Albert said, but went to Mister Johnny just the same and held out his hand. 'Come on, hand it over.'

Mister Johnny scowled and covered the skull with his hands.

Nick said, 'That's not the way to ask, Albert. It just makes him stubborn.' He slid off Hepzibah's lap. 'Look what I've got, Mister Johnny, look what I've got! My new knife. It's sharp as a razor, a real hunting knife, but if you keep the sheath on you can hold it a bit. If you give me that first.'

Mister Johnny looked at Nick; then he laughed and gave him the skull. Nick handed it to Carrie, behind him, and went on talking gently. 'You just stroke the leather, isn't it lovely and slippy? It's a beautiful knife. Mr Evans gave it to me and he gave Carrie a ring. D'you want Carrie to show you?'

Mister Johnny was too absorbed in the knife, running his finger along it to feel the pattern stamped out in the leather.

Hepzibah said, 'Show me, Carrie love.'

Carrie hadn't wanted to show her, in case Hepzibah should feel *she* ought to give them parting presents as well, but now there was no help for it. She put the skull down on the table, took the ring out of her pocket, and put it on her finger.

Hepzibah took her hand and bent her head over it. The little stone winked like a red star in the firelight and Carrie thought of Mrs Gotobed, suddenly; of the time she'd had tea with her and of the way the flames danced in her rings as she stroked the silk of her dress.

And because she was remembering that, when Albert said, 'It's *her* ring, isn't it?' she wasn't altogether surprised, only felt a little, shivery shock, as if something she had been half-expecting to happen, had happened at last.

Hepzibah's fingers tightened on hers. She said reluctantly, 'Well, very *like* it, perhaps,' and looked up at Carrie with what seemed a kind of apology.

'It *is*,' Albert said. 'It's her garnet ring! The one she wore most of the time.'

Carrie stood still. The blood drummed in her ears.

Hepzibah said, 'All right, Albert. Even if it did belong to her, it belongs to Mr Evans now, doesn't it?'

'He stole it,' Albert said.

'You can't steal what's your own! His sister's rings are his now, to keep or to give away as he chooses.' Hepzibah smiled at Carrie. 'I'm glad he gave it to you. Mrs Gotobed would be glad too, if she knew. So don't you pay any heed to Albert's old nonsense!'

Albert said, 'It's not nonsense. He *took* it then, if you don't like the word *steal*. Took it without saying anything. And he'd no right to do that, until it was all settled up. All the estate! That's the *law*, Hepzibah! I read it all up in the library.' He looked at Carrie and his eyes sparked with triumph. 'And if he took the ring, he might have taken something else, mightn't he?'

'That's enough, Mr Sea-Lawyer,' Hepzibah said.

'What's a sea laywer?' Nick asked, looking up.

'Someone who'll argue the hind leg off a donkey just for the sake of it. Now, d'you want that old story, or don't you? It's all one to me but time's getting on and your Auntie'll want you back early if you're to be up at crack of dawn in the morning.'

Carrie said slowly, 'I'll put the skull back first, shall I? In its box in the library.'

She wanted to be alone for a minute, away from Hepzibah's kindness and Albert's triumphant look. Of course, he'd been right all along! Mrs Gotobed had made a Will and Mr Evans had stolen it. Stolen it out of meanness and greed. He wanted Druid's Bottom and he didn't care what happened to Hepzibah and Mister Johnny. That was the worst thing, worse than stealing a ring, or even the Will. He didn't care about anyone; he'd turn Hepzibah out and live here himself, where he'd no right to be . . .

Carrie felt stifled. The library window was open and she went to stand by it, gulping in air. The evening breeze cooled her forehead and ruffled the surface of the horse pond in the yard. The horse pond was bottomless, Albert had said, when he threw the stone in.

Carrie's thoughts were like bits of a jigsaw, whirling round in her head. Separate pieces but all fitting in, one to another. Albert throwing a stone and it falling. Bombs falling on cities, houses crumbling like sand-castles. Horrible, but somehow exciting to think of. *Walls crumbling* – and the curse the African boy had put on Druid's Bottom if his skull ever left it. It had been taken out once and all the plates cracked, and the mirrors. Then they brought it back and the house had stood safe ever since, just so Mr Evans could live here and fill it with his meanness and greed. But the horse pond was bottomless . . .

Carrie lifted her arm and threw the skull as hard as she could. It sailed high, in an arc, then plopped into the pond. A few ripples, then nothing . . .

She stood, staring out at the pond and the dark Grove rising up the mountain behind it. She was shaking all over.

Albert said, behind her, 'What are you doing? Hepzibah's waiting.'

Had she sent him to comfort her? Carrie said, 'Nothing. I'm coming.'

She turned to face him and saw his glasses flash in the gloom.

He said awkwardly, 'It's all right, you know, Hepzibah's found a place. A farmer who wants a housekeeper and who'll take Mister Johnny. It's a bit bleak, she says, a hill farm, but it's good and remote and that's best for him. He'll be all right once he's settled.'

'Yes.' Carrie felt so tired. Like a piece of limp string.

Albert said, 'So all's well that ends well, you might say.'

Carrie said, 'D'you believe that?'

'I don't know.' He sounded ill at ease and she was terrified suddenly. Had he seen what she'd done? But all he said was, 'Let's be friends, Carrie,' and that was easy to answer.

She said, 'But we are friends, aren't we, Albert?'

Friends of course, and they promised to write. 'You write first,' Albert said. 'Care of Mr Morgan the Minister.'

Carrie laughed but he meant it. 'I shan't write till you do. And if you don't, I'll know, won't I?'

'Know what?' Carrie asked but he pulled a silly face and said nothing.

It was as if some queer shyness had seized him. When they left he didn't offer to walk them up through the Grove and Carrie wasn't sorry: she felt too chokey for talking.

'Mister Johnny will see you up to the ridge,' Hepzibah said, but Carrie shook her head.

'We'll be all right. I'm not scared any more.'

She wasn't scared; not even when she was half-way up the path, dark yews all round her, and heard the sound she had heard the first time. A soft, gentle sigh; a stirring and breathing . . .

Nick was some way ahead. Carrie stood still and listened but she wasn't afraid. It seemed a comforting sound now, as if the mountain had grown friendly towards her.

They ran along the railway line. 'We're late,' Carrie panted. 'I hope Auntie Lou won't be angry.'

'Oh no, she won't be angry,' Nick said. His eyes slid slyly sideways at Carrie and he started to giggle.

'I don't see what's funny,' Carrie said, and this set him off properly: he laughed so hard that he had to stop running. He doubled up and lurched about, clutching his stomach.

'For heaven's sake!' Carrie said. 'Of course she won't really be angry, I know *that*, silly fool! I only meant she might worry. And that 'ud be mean of us, wouldn't it? On our last night.'

She marched off and left him. He followed her at once, as she knew he would, and slipped his hand into hers. He said, very meekly, 'Honestly, Carrie, I don't think Auntie Lou will be worried.'

And she wasn't. Couldn't have been, because she wasn't at home. Lights were on everywhere; in the shop, in the passage, in the kitchen . . . 'Wasting electricity!' Carrie said, horrified. 'She must have gone mad! Good thing we got home before Mr Evans.'

She had left their supper ready on the kitchen table: a plate of bread and dripping covered with a cloth and a jug of milk with a note propped against it.

'That's for *him*,' Nick said, watching Carrie. He wrapped his arms round himself like a boy hugging a secret but he was so excited it came spilling out of him.

'She's gone,' he said. 'Gone with Major Cass Harper. They're getting married tomorrow.'

'You *knew*,' Carrie cried. 'Nicholas *Willow*! Why didn't you tell me? Oh, I could *hit* you!'

She doubled her fists and Nick laughed and dodged out of reach round the table. 'You might have told Mr Evans.'

'Oh, *Nick*! Did *she* think that? Was that why she told you and not me?'

He looked at her hurt face and stopped capering. 'Well, not really. And she didn't really tell me, it was just that I guessed, I'd seen them quite a few times, mooning about, and I asked her if she was going to marry him. She wouldn't say even then but I plagued her a bit till she couldn't keep it to herself any longer. She said, keep it dark, not meaning *you* mustn't know, but I thought – well, you know what you are! Sorry for him all the time. *Poor Mr Evans . . .*'

'I'm not sorry now,' Carrie said.

CHAPTER 14

*B*est to be in bed and out of the way before Mr Evans came home! What would he do, what would he say? The thought of it scared them so much they turned all the lights out and went straight upstairs without even taking a candle in case he came up and saw the light under their door. They undressed in the dark, in gathering panic, and fell into bed and closed their eyes tight and pretended to snore. He wouldn't wake them if he thought they were sleeping.

Carrie thought she would never be able to sleep, but she did – perhaps because she was pretending so hard – and slept deeply. So deeply and dreamlessly that when she woke she couldn't think at first where she was; nor place the strange noise at the back of her head. *Scrape,* rattle, *scrape*, rattle. Like rats scrabbling the other side of the wall.

No, not rats! She woke fully and knew that Mr Evans was home and riddling the fire. The noise always travelled like that, up the chimney.

She lay still, quaking a little to start with, at the thought of him sitting down there, angrily riddling the fire as if he were punishing it because his sister had left him, and then she began to feel angry herself. She thought of all the wicked things he had done and her anger grew and grew like a dark flower opening inside her. She had been sorry for him, and he had cheated her! He had given her a ring that didn't belong to him; a ring he had stolen as he had stolen Mister Johnny's safety and Hepzibah's happiness when he had stolen the will! There was nothing she could do about that, but she could give the ring back and that would show what she thought of him! Albert had said she was brave! Well, she would do a brave thing, for once. She would go straight downstairs, now this minute, and throw the ring back in his face!

She flew out of bed, out of the room, across the landing, down the stairs, treading as heavily as she could and wishing she had hobnailed boots on instead of bare feet! That would teach him, that would wear out his carpet!

A great wind of rage seemed to blow her along the passage, flung the doors open and then dropped her, becalmed, just inside it.

She breathed hard but said nothing. Mr Evans was

sitting there, staring at the dead fire, the poker in his hand. He looked up and saw her and said, in a puzzled voice, 'Bit early, isn't it?'

She said, 'Late you mean, don't you?' and looked at the clock on the mantelpiece. It was half past five in the morning.

Mr Evans said, 'I was just going to wake you. Train goes at seven.' He stood up, his bones creaking, and went to the kitchen window to take the blackout frame down. Light poured in and the sound of birds singing.

Carrie said, 'You been up all night?'

He nodded. He took the kettle from its hook above the fire and filled it at the sink. He hung it back in its place, then knelt to put screwed-up newspaper and kindling in the grate. When it flared up he put the coal on, small lump by small lump as Auntie Lou always did and as Carrie watched him, doing Auntie Lou's job, all the anger went out of her.

He said, 'Soon get it going. Cup of tea, bit of breakfast. Bacon, I thought. Fried bread and tomatoes. Something hot to set you up for the journey.'

Carried said, in a small voice, 'Not for Nick. The grease might upset him. He gets sick on trains.'

'Porridge, then.' He looked round, rather helplessly.

'I can do that,' Carrie said. She took the double saucepan from the rack and the packet of oats from the cupboard and busied herself, not looking at him.

She could feel him looking at *her*. His eyes on the back of her neck! But when she turned round, he was laying the table.

She said breathlessly, 'Auntie Lou . . .'

'Gone. Off with her fancy man. Did you know?'

She bit her lip till it hurt. 'Nick did. I didn't.'

He grunted, dropped a spoon and bent to pick it up. 'She's made her own bed. Much good may it do her!'

Carrie said, 'Are you – are you angry?'

He sucked his teeth thoughtfully. 'Ate a lot, your Auntie Lou did. Always at it, munch munch, nibble nibble, just like a rabbit. Now she's gone there'll be one less mouth to feed, one less mouth to eat up the profits. Fred will feel the benefit when he comes to take over the business.'

Carrie thought of Fred, standing in the hay field. Standing there and scowling and telling Mrs Gotobed that he wasn't coming back after the war, that he wasn't going into the shop . . .

Mr Evans said, 'Told the boy, did she? Why couldn't she tell me, then? Face to face? Instead of stealing away like a thief in the night! Just leaving a note! That does rile me, a bit!'

'Perhaps she was scared of what you might say,' Carrie suggested, and he snorted contemptuously.

'Scared? What's she got to be scared of me for? No – to make me look small, that's her object! Just like her fine sister, Dilys. The two of them make a right pair, sending messages, leaving notes – you look at this, now!' He turned to the mantelpiece, took a brown envelope from behind the clock, and shook something out, on to the table. 'An old photograph!' he said. 'That's all I had from Dilys on her death bed – and not even sent to me neither! I had to find it, going through her things and making a record as her grand London Lawyer instructed me!'

The photograph was brown and curling at the edges. It was a picture of a girl wearing a frilly bonnet and long, frilly drawers that reached down below her dress to her ankles. She was sitting in a chair, her feet on a footstool, and a boy in a sailor suit stood beside her. Both children had high, bony foreheads and pale, bulgy eyes.

Carrie said, 'Is that – is that you and Mrs Gotobed, then?'

He nodded and chewed at the side of this thumb. 'I'd be ten years, about. Dilys a bit older.'

Carrie stretched her mind to imagine Mr Evans being so young. Younger than she was now. Younger than *Nick*.

He said, 'Forty-five years ago. Long time, you'll be thinking it? Only other picture I've got of her, I keep in my watch.'

He took his old-fashioned fob watch out of his waistcoat pocket and clicked the back open. The girl in the photograph smiled out, rather older now, her hair in a bun, one hand touching her cheek. Mr Evans said, 'See that ring she's got on? That's the one you've got now. I bought it for her, see, with my first wages, and when she gave it back, I gave it to you. So there's a bit of old history you've got with that ring.'

Carrie swallowed hard. 'When she gave it back?'

'Don't parrot, girl! You heard me! It was with the

picture. No letter, nothing – just my name on the envelope tucked away in her jewel box.'

'Nothing else *at all*?' It was hard to ask, but she had to make sure.

'What else should there be?' He looked suspiciously at her. 'What are you grinning for?'

'I'm just glad,' Carrie said, and she was. Glad to know he wasn't a bad man, not a thief, after all. But she could hardly tell him that! She said, 'I'm glad she sent them back, the ring and the picture. It meant she remembered, didn't it, that she'd thought of you?'

'Seemed more like a slap in the face to me,' he said. 'But take it your way, if you like. Now you get upstairs double quick and wake up that idle young brother of yours, or you'll be missing your train.'

He came to the station and saw them into the carriage. He said, 'You'll be all right now. No point in my waiting.'

He didn't kiss them good-bye but he touched Carrie's cheek and ruffled Nick's hair. 'Young Nicodemus,' he said, and turned on his heel.

'Well, that's over,' Nick said, and sat back.

'Don't be mean,' Carrie said. 'He was quite nice at the end.'

'*Nice?*' Nick rolled his eyes upwards.

'Not so bad, then.' She wished she could tell him that Mr Evans hadn't stolen the Will after all, but Nick had never thought that he had, so there was no point in it. And there was no chance to tell Albert. She had half hoped he would be at the station but there was no sign of him.

She said, 'I wonder if Albert'll be waving up on the line. I would, if I was him.'

'This time of the morning?' Nick said.

Carrie sighed.

'We can wave to the house, though,' Nick said. 'There's a place where you can see it, after the bend.'

'I shan't look,' Carrie said. 'I don't think I can bear to.'

She leaned back and closed her eyes. She felt tired already, though the day had hardly begun.

Nick said, 'When can we open our lunch packet, Carrie? My stomach's *flapping*.'

She ignored that remark. She sat, feigning sleep: she had decided to keep her eyes closed all the way to the junction. And when the train started she wished she could close her ears too, because Nick stood at the window and sang, 'Good-bye town, good-bye. Good-bye War Memorial, good-bye square. Good-bye Chapel on Sundays. Good-bye old slag heap . . .'

Carrie thought, *my heart's breaking* . . .

'Good-bye mountain, good-bye trees,' Nick chanted as the train gathered speed.

Carrie felt she couldn't bear to hear that light, cheerful voice sing out, 'Good-bye, Druid's Bottom.' She jumped up and thrust him down on the seat, holding his shoulders. He said, squirming, 'Let me go, Carrie, let me go, rotten beast,' and she laughed and released him and turned to the window . . .

And screamed. The train whistle blew at the same moment and her scream was drowned in it. Nick only saw her dark, open mouth and her eyes, shocked and staring.

He stumbled up and she clung to him. The train whistled once more and shot into the tunnel.

Nick felt Carrie shaking and shuddering. The train joggled and they fell on the seat, clasped together. She said, in the dark in the tunnel, 'It's on fire, Nick. Druid's Bottom on *fire*. Blazing away, flames and smoke – they'll all be dead, Nick . . .' She started to cry. She said, between sobs that seemed to tear her chest open, something that sounded like, 'All my fault . . .' He knew it couldn't be that because it didn't make sense but there was no point in asking her what she had said because she was crying too hard.

She cried and cried and Nick sat and watched. He didn't know how to stop her and when she did stop by herself, when they got to the junction and had to change trains, he was afraid to say anything in case she started again, and so he said nothing. Neither then, nor later: Carrie never mentioned Druid's Bottom after that day, not to him, nor to their mother, and because she had frightened him so badly, crying like that, neither did he.

CHAPTER 15

*E*ven thirty years later, when she was quite old enough to know it wasn't her fault, that a house didn't burn down because a girl threw a skull into a horse pond, she still cried in much the same way when she thought of it. Not in front of the children but later, when they had all gone to bed and to sleep. Only the oldest boy stayed awake and he heard her, crying softly in the next room. On and on, like a waterfall . . .

In the morning he told the others they were not to disturb her. She was tired, he said; they would go for a walk before breakfast and let her sleep as long as she needed.

He knew where he was going. He led them at a smart pace along the path where the railway had been and though they grumbled about the branches scratching their legs his sister and his brothers followed him. But when they came to the Grove, they stopped and hung back.

He said, 'You don't have to come. None of you.'

That made them want to, of course. And they were not really the sort of children who were easily frightened. Once they had set their feet on the path they tumbled down bold and bouncy as puppies.

Carrie's daughter said, 'What were they scared of, her and Uncle Nick? Just a few silly old trees!'

But when they got to the bottom of the Grove they were scared a little. The ruined house looked so dead in the sunlight with its blackened walls and boarded-up windows. There was the yard and the horse pond – and the dead house beyond them.

'Come on,' the oldest boy said. 'We can't just go back. Might as well have a proper look, while we're here.'

But even he went forward slowly. The smallest one clung to him. 'Were they really all burned up? To a *cinder*?'

'She thought so.'

'Why didn't she ask someone?'

'Scared to find out, I suppose.'

'Scaredy-cat. She's a scaredy-cat!'

'You'd be too, I expect, if you'd done what she did,' the oldest boy said. 'Or thought you had. Let me see, the stables must be round at the side.'

They turned the corner of the house and saw what looked like an outbuilding, only rather a smart one, painted white and with a tub of nasturtiums outside the open front door. Carrie's daughter wrinkled her nose. 'Bacon cooking?'

'Ssh . . .' The oldest boy seized the younger two and dragged them back, out of sight. 'If someone's living there we've no business to go rootling round. Trespassing.'

'I didn't see any notice to stop us,' Carrie's daughter said. She peered round the corner of the house. Then flapped her hands behind her. 'Hang *on* . . .' They waited. When she turned round, her cheeks were fat as balloons, fit to burst. She blew out through her lips and pretended to fan herself. She said, 'How *old* was Hepzibah?'

'I don't know. Mum didn't say.'

'She didn't say nothing about people's ages.'

'*Didn't* she?'

'Don't know. Can't remember.'

'What are you whispering for?' the oldest boy said. He looked himself and saw a tall old woman coming towards them. No, not towards *them* – she didn't know they were there – towards a gate that led to a field tucked away under the mountain. A flash of white feathers in the field, and the old woman was carrying a bucket. Hepzibah! Hepzibah going to feed her chickens! Even if it isn't, he thought, she can't bite me!

He stepped out of cover and walked up to her. She had grey eyes and white hair. He said, speaking fast to get it over with, but politely, 'Are you Miss Hepzibah Green? If you are, my mother remembers you.'

She stared at him. Stared and stared — and her grey eyes seemed to grow larger and brighter. At last she said, 'Carrie? Carrie's boy?'

He nodded, and her eyes shone brilliant as diamonds. Her face cracked in a thousand lines when she smiled. 'And the others?'

'Yes.'

'Gracious Heavens!'

She looked at them all, one by one, then again at the oldest boy. 'You look like your mother. They don't, but you do.'

'Green eyes,' he said. 'It's having green eyes.'

'Not only that.' She looked at him, smiling, and he thought she was beautiful, even though she was old and had a stiff, curly whisker or two on her chin. The little ones would giggle at that if they noticed, and if they giggled she'd know what about, he was sure. She was *sharp*. He thought, I'd better warn them . . .

She said, 'What am I thinking about? You'll be wanting your breakfast and here I am, standing here as if eggs cooked themselves. White ones or brown ones? Or speckledy?'

'Oh, we don't want . . .' he began, but she was leading the way; very tall, very thin, very old; skinny old legs stiff as stilts.

They went in through the white painted door, down a passage into a kitchen. It had been part of a barn perhaps, because there was a high ceiling and beams but it was cosy and bright, with a wood fire in the hearth and the sun streaming in.

Hepzibah said. 'Look who's here, Mister Johnny! Carrie's children!'

He sat in a chair in the sun by the window; a tiny bald man, like an elderly goblin. He blinked at them sleepily.

'Say hallo to Carrie's children,' Hepzibah said.

He smiled shyly, ducking his head. 'Hayo, hayo. How you?'

'He can speak!' Carrie's daughter said. 'He can speak properly!' Her face swelled with rage at the thought of the lies her mother had told.

'Not when Carrie was here, he couldn't,' Hepzibah said. 'After the war, when Albert was grown, he had a friend of his, a speech therapist, come down from London. Mister Johnny will never talk like the rest of us, but it's more company for me, having him answer, and it's better for him. He doesn't feel so cut off. Your mother tell you about Albert?'

They nodded.

'Albert Sandwich! What a name!' Hepzibah stood with her eyes fixed on distance, remembering. 'Oh, they were a pair, him and your mother! Talk of opposites! Mr Head and Miss Heart, I used to call them, and both of them stubborn as mules when their minds were fixed. *She* said she'd write first, he said, and nothing would budge him. Mr Cocksure, he seemed sometimes, but he was shy underneath. He thought she couldn't be bothered, once she'd gone away.'

'She thought he was dead, that's why she never wrote,' the oldest boy said. 'She thought you were all dead, in the fire.' *How absurd,* he thought, *did she really think that?*

'How did she know about the old fire?'

'She saw it from the train.'

Hepzibah looked at him. *Witch's eyes,* the oldest boy thought. But that was ridiculous! He said, 'She threw the skull in the horse pond. She thought she'd started the fire, doing that. It sounds silly now.'

Hepzibah said, 'Poor little Carrie!' She looked at him. 'She believed my old tales. You wouldn't, would you?'

'No, I don't think so.' But her bright eyes seemed to be seeing more than eyes usually did, seeing straight into him, and it made him less certain. He said, 'I don't know.'

She said, 'The insurance people said it was Mister Johnny, playing with matches. All *I* know is, it was him woke us up. Saved our lives, probably. Nothing else, though Albert got a few old books out of the library – burned his hands and his eyebrows off! He looked a real scarecrow!'

'Was all the house burned?'

'Gutted inside. The floors and the staircase. We moved into the barn – camped out, to begin with. Then the lawyers did up the outbuildings and said we could stay on as caretakers. Keep an eye on what was left of the place.'

'What happened to Mr Evans?' Carrie's daughter said. 'It all belonged to him, didn't it?'

'He died, poor man. Not long after the fire. Heart, the doctors said, but it was more grief and loneliness. Missed his sister – she'd left him to marry an American soldier.'

'*Auntie Lou?*'

'That's what Carrie and Nick used to call her. Mrs Cass Harper, that's her name now. She went to live in North Carolina, after the war. We heard nothing from her for years till last summer, when her son came down to have a look at the place. Tall young man with a drawly voice – hard to make head or tail of what he said, really.'

'Schewgullum,' Mister Johnny said, looking excited.

'That's right. Brought Mister Johnny some chewing gum and he got it stuck to his dentures! Albert came to meet young Mr Harper and fixed up to buy the place. He says he wants to re-build and live here one day but I think he was thinking more of Mister Johnny and me. You'll be safe now, he said when the papers were signed, no one can turn you out, ever! And we're grateful, of course, though he won't hear of gratitude! He says we're all the family he's got, since his own parents died when he was a little lad, and he's got no one else, never married. Oh, he's been like a son to us, Albert has! Comes down at least once a month. Due this weekend, as a matter of fact . . .'

All the time she was talking, she was setting the table with egg cups and mugs, and cutting bread and butter. Eggs were boiling on the stove; she lifted them out and said, 'Come on now, you must be hungry.'

The eggs were beautiful; firm whites and dark, runny yolks. And the butter, thickly spread on crisp bread, was like no butter they had ever tasted: smooth, but leaving a grainy, salt tang behind on the tongue.

'Was Albert an orphan then?' Carrie's daughter asked. '*She* didn't say!'

'Who's *she*? The cat's mother?'

'No, mine,' she said, grinning at Hepzibah.

'Little Carrie,' Hepzibah said in her soft, remembering voice, and this made the children laugh.

'She's ever so tall for a woman,' the oldest boy said. 'Our dad used to call her a bean pole.'

He felt Hepzibah's eyes on him and buried his face in his mug. He had said *used to*! Would Hepzibah start poking and prying? Most people did and he hated it – hated having to explain that his father was dead. But Hepzibah wasn't 'most people', he realized suddenly. She hadn't once asked any of the ordinary questions. 'Where is your mother?' 'What are you doing here, by yourselves?' 'Does she know where you are?'

Hepzibah said thoughtfully, 'It'll be good to see little Carrie. She may have grown taller, but she's the sort doesn't change other ways. Nor your Uncle Nick, neither. How is he, now?'

'Fat,' the little ones said and looked at each other and giggled.

'Well, he always had an eye for his stomach. Mister Johnny, d'you remember Nick? How that boy used to eat!'

Mister Johnny looked blank.

'It's a long time for him to remember a name,' Hepzibah said. 'Though he'd know Nick at once if he saw him, he doesn't forget those he loves. He'll know Carrie when she comes. Does she still like her eggs boiled five minutes?'

The children sat quiet. Then the oldest boy said, 'She won't come, Hepzibah. I mean, she'll come when we go back and fetch her, but she's not coming *now*. She's too – too afraid . . .'

Had always been afraid, he thought. More afraid than most mothers. Not stopping them doing things, she wasn't silly like that, but you would look at her sometimes and see the fear, holding her still. Especially when they were happy. As if she were afraid of a happy time stopping.

He thought, perhaps because *this* happy time had come to an end all those years ago, and she blamed herself for it . . .

Hepzibah was smiling at him as if she knew what he was thinking: as if she understood everything. But she couldn't understand – she was just a clever old woman who had persuaded Carrie to believe her old tales. Hepzibah had taken his mother in with her spooky nonsense, the oldest boy thought, and felt, all at once, rather indignant.

Hepzibah turned to the stove and put a brown egg in the simmering water. 'That'll be timed about right,' she said. 'You go and meet her. Tell her all's well and her egg's on the boil and Hepzibah's waiting. Run along quickly, she'll be half down the mountain by now!'

Her voice had a clear command in it and the children stood up and went meekly out of the kitchen, past the old, ruined house, past the horse pond . . .

As they crossed the yard the oldest boy stopped being indignant with Hepzibah and felt sorry instead because she was so foolishly sure and was going to be disappointed. She thought she knew their mother was coming, and she couldn't possibly know! She wasn't a witch; just an old woman who was quite good at guessing, but had guessed wrong, this time.

'There's no point in hanging about,' he said. 'We'll wait a minute to please Hepzibah and then we'll go back and finish our breakfast. I daresay one of us can eat an extra egg!'

But the others were younger than he was and so still believing, still trusting. They looked at him, then at each other, and laughed.

And ran ahead to meet their mother, coming through the Druid's Grove.

AFTERWORD

Nina Bawden was fourteen when the Second World War broke out. Like many children living in London she was evacuated from the dangers of bombing to the comparative safety of a Welsh mining community where she lived with several different families, including a chemist and his wife who lived above the shop, as do Mr Evans and Auntie Lou in *Carrie's War*.

'As Nina Bawden explains: '*Carrie's War* is loosely based on my wartime experiences. Carrie, who is twelve, and her younger brother Nick, leave London in a darkened train as I did, labelled like parcels. I remember asking my teacher why we had to have labels and she said that if the train was bombed and we were blown to bits, the labels might help to identify our bodies. I think I asked too many questions altogether and she was fed up with me. Carrie's story is not mine, but her feelings about being away from home for the first time are ones I remember. I had a photograph of my mother with me. So did the children in *Carrie's War*, but they don't look at it much. It was a good likeness of their mother and she was smiling at them, but she didn't belong there. Like their father . . . she belonged somewhere else. In a dream, in another life.'

Carrie and Nick are taken in by the kindly Auntie Lou, who is as lovely as she dares to be with her tyrannical brother Mr Evans breathing down her neck. Carrie adapts quickly to the quirky nature of their home and even Nick, who misses his real home far more, settles into the ways of a Welsh village and the Evans' household.

Nowadays it seems astonishing that parents were willing to let their children go and stay far away from home with complete strangers. For many of the children it was understandably a bewildering and frightening time. They lost the emotional security of family life as well as coming face to face with the country, which many had never even visited before. But for some there were compensations. As an evacuee herself, Nina Bawden obviously understands all of those feelings and her story gives an emotional rather than historical insight into the war years.

Although Carrie and Nick suffer from homesickness, their new home soon has a reality which makes their real home shadowy in comparison. On balance *Carrie's War* is not just about how the children survive the upheaval of evacuation. It is more about how some can thrive and grow on it. As in many of the best stories for children the absence of parents enables the children to do all kinds of things that would not be possible if they were properly supervised. For Nina Bawden herself this was certainly true. She says: 'We shared a school with the local children, using the building alternate mornings and afternoons, and attending other lessons in various church halls and Welsh Nonconformist chapels. The distance between these makeshift class-

rooms gave us more freedom than most of us had ever
had before. It was easy to get 'lost' between Ebenezer
and Elijah – I did Latin in one, History in the other. If
more of us turned up to our classes than might have
been expected in the circumstances, this may have been
because we were a biddable generation, or simply that
there was little alternative amusement on offer in the
Welsh mining valleys. But for girls of thirteen to
sixteen, the sense of not being watched, *brooded over*
by concerned adults, was heady. 'Uncles' and 'Aunties'
could be tiresome, but there was none of the usual
emotional tension between adolescents and their real
parents. No one bothered with us much, except our
teachers occasionally, and even they had more important things to think about. There was a war on after
all.'

Carrie, like Nina Bawden, makes the most of this
lack of supervision. Not just to be places where she
perhaps should not be but, more importantly, to think
in ways that she would not have done had she stayed
at home. Without any guidance as to how to judge
people she makes up her own mind and, in so doing,
gives a perceptive if bemused picture of the community
in which she is living. But Carrie gets out of her depth
when she starts to interpret the stories the kindly Hepzi-
bar tells, and she carries away from her war years a
strong sense of guilt which she cannot overcome until
she takes her own children back and, in so doing, pieces
the story together from her adult point of view.

Carrie's War is a book of enormous insight into how

children adapt to strange surroundings; how well they are able to think for themselves, yet, how easy it is for them to distort facts and, in so doing, to create fictions which are frighteningly credible.

Julia Eccleshare

WATERSHIP DOWN
Richard Adams

Fiver felt sure that something terrible was going to happen to the warren – and Fiver's sixth sense was never wrong.

Yet the fleeing band of rabbits could never have imagined the terrors and dangers they were to encounter in their search for a new home.

TOM'S MIDNIGHT GARDEN
Philippa Pearce

Sent to stay with his aunt and uncle in a dull old house without even a garden, Tom is not looking forward to his summer holiday.

But when the clock strikes thirteen at midnight, Tom opens a door to find an adventure more wonderful than he ever could have imagined.

STIG OF THE DUMP
Clive King

One glorious day the ground gives way beneath Barney and he lands in a cave in the middle of the rubbish dump; and that's when he meets Stig.

Nobody believes his story, but for Barney Stig is totally real, and together they embark on a series of wonderful adventures.

THE SILVER SWORD
Ian Serraillier

This is the story of four children's struggle to stay alive throughout the years of Nazi occupation and, afterwards, their epic journey from war-torn Poland to Switzerland in search of their parents.

Based on a true story, this is an extraordinarily moving account of life during and after the Second World War.

THE MOUSE AND HIS CHILD
Russell Hoban

Once they are bought and leave the safety of the toy
shop, the clockwork mouse and his child begin their
search for the beautiful doll's house they had once
known.

But, always on their track, determined to destroy
them, is the evil Manny Rat.

CHARLOTTE'S WEB
E. B. White

This is the story of a little girl called Fern who loves a
little pig called Wilbur. And of how Wilbur's dear
friend Charlotte A. Cavatica, a beautiful grey spider,
saves Wilbur from the usual fate of nice fat pigs, by a
wonderfully clever plan (which no one else could
possibly have thought of).

BALLET SHOES
Noel Streatfeild

Adopted as babies by Great Uncle Matthew, Pauline, Petrova and Posy Fossil lead a sheltered life until they begin at the Children's Academy of Dancing and Stage Training.

Only then do they begin to discover their special talents and extraordinary ambitions.

SMITH
Leon Garfield

Smith was a pickpocket – and a very accomplished one at twelve years old.

But the instant he empties the pockets of a certain old gentleman, he finds himself caught up in a dangerous web of murder, intrigue and betrayal.

THE BORROWERS
Mary Norton

Pod, Homily and Arrietty are a family of tiny people who live beneath the floor, behind the kitchen clock. Everything they have is borrowed from the 'human beans' who don't even know they exist.

That is, until the fateful day when Arrietty makes friends with 'the boy upstairs'.